A beautiful and engrossing tale of a mighty child, a magnificent forest and the mysteries which bind us all in the best ways – this is a rich and powerful book, a real triumph of love, wisdom and storytelling.

Horatio Clare

Bigfoot Mountain transports readers into the heart of the forest and allows them to see the wild from the perspective of the beings who know it best. A skilful interweaving of modern family relationships and wilderness adventure.

Nicola Davies

An innovative and moving story, filled with wonderful descriptions of the West Coast wilderness.

Tyler Keevil

A compelling story of courage, protecting nature and finding your way.

Erin Hamilton

D0278198

To my children, Augustus and Oona

BIGFOOT MOUNTAIN

First published in 2021
by Firefly Press
25 Gabalfa Road, Llandaff North, Cardiff, CF14 2JJ
www.fireflypress.co.uk

© Roderick O'Grady 2021

The author asserts his moral right to be identified as author in
accordance with the Copyright, Designs and Patent Act, 1988.

All rights reserved.
This book is sold subject to the condition that it shall not, by way of
trade or otherwise, be lent, re-sold, hired out or otherwise circulated
without the publisher's prior consent in any form, binding or cover
other than that in which it is published and without a similar
condition including this condition being imposed on the
subsequent purchaser.

All characters in this publication are fictitious and any resemblance
to real persons, living or dead, is purely coincidental.

A CIP catalogue record of this book is available from
the British Library.

1 3 5 7 9 8 6 4 2

ISBN 978-1-913102-41-8
ebook ISBN 978-1-913102-42-5

This book has been published with the support of the
Books Council of Wales.

Typeset by: Elaine Sharples
Cover and internal illustration by Jess Mason,
www.jessmasonillustration.com

Printed and bound by CPI Group UK

BIGFOOT
MOUNTAIN

RODERICK O'GRADY

Firefly

BIGFOOT MOUNTAIN

MINNIE

Chapter One

High, high, high up in a pine tree, where the slopes of a mountain meet the shoreline of a bay, sat Minnie. She sat on her branch hugging the slender top of the trunk as the wind gently swayed her tree back and forth. She loved the scent from the pine needles and the thin dribbles of sap that wept from the tree and made her hands sticky as she climbed, and she loved meeting the ants and centipedes and spiders and all the other bugs that lived in its lumpy, scaly bark. A fly landed on her freckly nose. She waved it away.

Minnie twisted on her perch and, shading her eyes from the sun, peered up at the forested mountain and the pale grey cloud of smoke that filled half the blue sky behind it.

On the far side of the water a dark, glowering cloud loomed over the tree-covered hills. There was a sudden *flash*, followed a second later by a loud *crack!* She watched as a jagged three-pronged fork flashed to the ground, striking the highest point of the long green hilly island that lay close to the opposite shore. A second later there came a deep, grumbling roll of thunder.

She noticed a distant silhouette of a bird wheeling and arching high above. The bird turned towards Minnie gliding on the warm air. It was a golden eagle. As it flew overhead, she could see splashes of white on the under side of its wings, the black-and-white fanned tail, and the bright yellow talons that looked ever ready to grasp a fish straight out of the water or to snatch a weasel from the long grass.

Minnie stared at the mass of dense green trees on the far island, wondering if there would be a burst of flames, wondering what lightning did when it hit. She imagined a tree exploding in bits in a flash and all the animals that lived in or near it running or flying away in a desperate panic. Nature could be cruel, she thought, and she looked down at her home, her little cabin in the clearing by the bay, surrounded by many, many square miles of nothing but water, trees and more trees.

There were six cabins dotted among the pine trees on the cleared land between the grassy track and the shore, plus one more up the track near the forest. Minnie and Dan's cabin was nestled in tight between a rocky outcrop and the vegetable garden, which had a high fence all round it to keep deer and other wild animals out. It overlooked their five cabins, which were all built raised up on stout posts, high enough for storage space under them, with wooden steps up to a wide deck.

Her stepfather, Dan, was coming down the steps of their cabin carrying a can of paint and a ladder. From up in her tree Dan looked very tiny as he walked across the grass from their cabin to the next one. Minnie reckoned if she was standing on the ground looking down at a daisy, with its white petals and yellow centre, that's about how big Dan looked now.

Up above the world Minnie felt calm, and connected to something big and important. She didn't know what that was exactly, but guessed it was nature as she was in a tree rooted to the earth and through the tree she was connected to the whole world. And though her mom had gone, Minnie felt less alone when she was hugging her tree.

Minnie climbed down from the pine, and as she did so some of her hair snagged on the lowest branch. 'Ow! Darn hair!' Her hair was a mass of light brown curls so unruly that it was impossible to play hide-and-go-seek outside in the bushes behind the cabins unless she was wearing a beanie hat pulled down low, or she would quickly get entangled and have to yell for her friend Billy to come and release her, and that would defeat the purpose of the game since Billy was the only other person playing with her. One time her hair got so caught up that Billy had to go get her mother to cut her free with a pair of scissors. It was annoying.

The grass between the cabins was short and neat and the scent of its freshly mown greenness lifted her spirits. Minnie kicked off her shoes so she could enjoy the warmth and softness of the grass on her feet and strolled over to Dan.

'Where've you been?' Dan asked, 'I saw the school bus twenty minutes ago.'

'Nowhere. What ya doin'?' Dan didn't answer so Minnie said, 'I was up a tall tree watching the lightning strike the island. Lightning, Dan! And

wondering whether it was going to strike me next.'
Still nothing from Dan. 'It did not, you'll be
pleased to hear. What ya doin'?'

'How was school?' he asked.

'Fine. What ya doin'?'

'What does it look like I'm doing?'

Minnie answered, 'Painting the cabins the same
boring colour they've always been. White!'

'Good enough for your mom for ten years, good
enough for me.'

'What's wrong with yellow? Or blue? How about
a different colour for each cabin? Then you could
say to the guests "Oh good afternoon, Lord and
Lady Snuffington, you are in the yellow cabin,
down there". "Oh," she'd say, "thank you, kind sir,
but how will I find it, as I'm rather dim and I have
people to help me in the big city?" And you'd say,
"It's yellow! Right next to the blue one!" Yes, it's a
brilliant idea, I agree, Dan, we could have yellow,
purple, blue, green and…'

Dan put down the tin of white paint, scratched
his black-and-silver beard, and looked at her while
she thought.

'And pink!'

'Best to leave well enough alone.' This was a

typical Dan response to Minnie trying to cheer him up with her particular brand of creative humour.

'Look, Dan! A plane. You love planes.' A white plane with big black propellers flew low over the water on the far side of the bay. It looked like it was going to land on the water but instead skimmed over the surface, sending up a white plume of spray from its belly before taking off again. 'What's it doin'?' asked Minnie.

'Taking on water. That's the Bombadier 415, also known as the Super Scooper. It can take on 6,000 litres of water in twelve seconds, and…'

They watched the plane lift and soar high in the sky, turning toward the mountain. '…and then it's gonna dump that water on the fire.'

'Fascinating, Dan, but I thought you said the fire was out now.'

'It is. I think. They've been using helicopters to dump water. I guess the plane was busy elsewhere.' Dan looked up at the mountain behind the cabins. 'We could do with rain. I heard thunder.'

'That was on the other side of the bay,' said Minnie, pointing at the island. 'So, Dan, why do they need the plane to drop water if it's gonna rain?'

'That rain might just blow north and miss us.'

Minnie looked to the thunderclouds and then back to the plane, which was now about the same size in the sky as the eagle was when it flew over.

'If the fire's out, why are the cabins still empty?'

'Fire danger. State told us to cancel all bookings. That was when the fire was spreading. Besides no one wants to come when there's wild fires.'

'So, are we screwed?'

'*Screwed*? That is not appropriate language for a twelve year old to be using.'

'Oh. OK,' said Minnie, 'but *are* we?'

'No, business is fine.' He picked up the paint can. 'Well, it'll pick up.' And he walked off towards the next empty cabin.

Chapter Two

Inside their cabin, the cabin where she had been born and where her mother had died, Minnie stood in the kitchen drinking a glass of water. Since her mother had passed, the weekends were long and uneventful. She had books and she had the internet but she had always loved exploring with her mom best of all. When the sea was calm, they'd go canoeing together, along the shore exploring the dozens of small islands. Some were big enough to build a cabin on, and some had just one or two low bent trees growing on them.

Using their paddles, they'd scoop up the dark red spiny sea urchins from the shallows, some the size of a soccer ball. To Minnie they looked despairing and lost just waving their long, thin, scarlet spikes around helplessly. She would drop them back in the water, in the deep rock pools.

Sometimes they'd trail a line behind the canoe and catch fish – pink salmon, or grey trout. They would take them home and cook them in hot butter. The three of them would eat at the small wooden table by the fire, and her mom would always say, without fail, 'Mmm, them's good eats!' They pulled the flesh from the bones and wolfed it down with chunks of the soft brown bread her mom would bake.

Minnie palmed tears from her cheeks and opened the door to her mom's room. She looked in the wardrobe and the scent from her mother's clothes enveloped her. How long would her clothes retain that smell? It was a combination of her mom's fancy French scent, which she insisted was called 'Optimist' although the bottle said something else, of wool from her sweaters, and leather from her belts and boots. Dan hadn't moved her clothes or put any of her things in storage. It was exactly how her mom had left it when she went to the hospital.

When she came home from the hospital, because she insisted on being in the place she loved most for her final days, she hadn't had the strength to open the wardrobe and she was done with clothes anyway. She'd said, 'I'm done with everything except love. Love for you, Minnie, and love for Dan. Love for my friends and love for this place. I need nothing else but love to send me on my way.'

Minnie decided to go and find Billy and Musto, because they were always 'up' and never 'down'. Billy and Minnie had something in common as, like her, he had just one grown-up looking after him, because his dad was always away driving trucks.

Instead of climbing out of the small bathroom window at the back of the cabin, which she usually did to save time, or going into the vegetable garden and climbing over the fence, she took the longer way round. She walked past her favourite tree, through the grassy car-parking area, and up the track. It led her past the solar panels Dan had installed on the rise behind their cabin, and past the wind turbine up on the little rocky outcrop close to the forest edge. Sitting on top of a tall metal post, supported by cables pegged to the ground, were four slim white blades, like an aeroplane's propeller, which turned steadily in a breeze, generating electricity for the cabins.

Billy and his mom, Connie, lived in the seventh cabin, on a small parcel of land up the track a ways, close to the forest, and as it was higher up the slope it had a clear view over the cabins and across the bay. Connie had bought the land from Minnie's mother, and the two women had built the cabin together. It was long and low, with flowering white honeysuckle curling and coiling in and along the wooden rails that bordered the front of the deck. Dan was hammering something somewhere as Minnie climbed the steps. From this high point she could see him on the roof of one of the cabins. Behind him stretched the blue-grey expanse of the bay framed by tall dark pines on both sides of the cabin clearing.

A shaggy-coated, yellow-tan dog lay on the deck and he lifted his head and wagged his tail, which thwacked on the wooden boards.

'Hey Musto,' she knelt, patting and stroking the dog. She yelled out, 'Billy-Bug!'

Minnie sometimes called him Billy-Bug because when her mother first saw the very tiny baby Billy wrapped up tightly in a blanket, she'd said, 'Oh don't he just look as snug as a bug in rug!' And he did. Her mom had called him that ever since.

The screen door was flung open by Connie. 'Hi Minnie. How are you doing?' She held a large wooden bowl of long, gnarly green beans.

'Hi Connie, I'm fine. Can Billy come play?'

A single bolt of silver ran through Connie's long

black-braided hair, fastened with a brown leather lace and with feathers pushed in to the knot. She was bare-footed, wearing a long, loose-fitting sky blue cotton frock. She put the bowl on the table.

'Let me give you a big hug.' She wrapped up Minnie in her arms and squeezed her tight.

'Stop it! Connie, stop it!'

'Oh, Minnie. Look at you. Growing so fast into a fine-looking young lady!'

Minnie wriggled free of Connie's arms.

'We saw each other yesterday, Connie!'

Billy appeared at the door, grinning cheerfully. He was ten and small for his age, with an unruly mop of straw-blond hair.

'I know but I just, I just…' Connie's hazel eyes welled up, 'I just, I feel for you so, for you both. How's Dan today?'

'Hard to know.'

'Uh huh. Strong silent type,' said Connie.

'Silent? He's perfected silence,' said Minnie, still petting Musto, 'except when he's hammering. He does a lot of hammering.'

They all three looked over at Dan, crouched over, hammering on the cabin roof.

'Well,' said Connie, 'good news about the fire

12

being out. Most folk here rely on summer takings to see 'em through winter.'

'Sure, yup, I know,' said Minnie, lifting up Musto's large floppy ears so the dog looked alert yet foolish.

'Your mom loved this place so much, Minnie. Well, we all do. How could we not?'

'Because there's no ice-cream parlour?' said Billy, making Minnie laugh.

'She'd walk in the woods for hours,' said Connie.

'Would she?' asked Minnie.

'Sure, while you were at school. Where d'you think she foraged all those mushrooms and shoots and herbs?'

'Huh,' said Minnie. 'Right.'

Connie started shucking the bowl of greens by twisting the pods so they split, then running a thumb up inside to dislodge the purple beans sitting there in a neat row. Minnie was mesmerised by this speed-shucking. Connie was so quick at it she barely looked at the beans as she worked and talked.

'Can be mighty lonely when there's no guests here though. Like in wintertime. I'm beginning to dread the winters, Minnie, I don't mind telling you. But my, this is such a beautiful place. I will never tire of that view. Never.' For maybe the millionth time in their lives the three of them turned to look out at the bay dotted with forested islands, carved apart by narrow channels and tidal passages.

'What's the big island called? Does it have a name, Connie?' asked Minnie.

'Um, let me think now. Echo. Echo Island,' said Connie. 'Looks like rain over there, but it might pass northerly.'

'I like the winter,' said Minnie. 'I like the snow. Without the winter we wouldn't love the spring so much.'

Billy leapt off the deck, tumbling into a forward roll and stopping in a kneeling position, holding his stick like a rifle.

'Let's go fishin'!' yelled Billy, and he charged off down the track. Musto bounded off the deck after Billy.

Minnie ran after them as Connie hollered, 'Be careful!'

Minnie grabbed Billy's arm. 'Billy-Bug.'
'What?'
'Let's go up.'
'Up what? Up where? What do you mean? Up? No.'

'Billy, look at me,' she said. 'What is your role in life?'

'Huh?' he asked.

'What do you see as your role in life, what's your main job, what do we expect of you?'

Billy looked up and around, genuinely perplexed by the question his friend was posing.

'OK … It is…' he began, 'it is to make you laugh as much as I can.'

'Thanks, but what else?' asked Minnie.

'To keep Mom safe,' he answered.

'What else?'

With a rising inflection he asked, 'Is it … to do as I'm *told*?'

'Correct!' Minnie pointed up at the forest. 'I wanna see the smoke! Up close.'

'Are you *crazy*? That's like a fifty-mile hike! Besides the fire's out.'

'I know the fire's out, but there's still smoke. I can see it from my tree. Dan says it's two miles to the top if you take the trails. So, gotta be less if you head straight up.'

Billy pondered this logic. 'Less if you head straight up…' He scratched his blond head. 'OK.'

'Good! You and me, up there! I have water.' She

hoisted her small red backpack onto her thin shoulders.

'Smoke!' Billy yelled, running straight up the trail towards the towering redwoods, pines and firs.

Chapter Three

They walked up the dusty hiking trail, hemmed in by dense forest either side. 'Let's cut up here,' said Minnie and she jumped off the main trail and shot up a much smaller 'game trail'. It was just a gap between scrubby low bushes and tall green grass made by animals pushing through the underbrush.

Musto bounded on ahead. Their feet crunched on dry leaves and sticks that had dropped from the pine trees and redwoods around them. Stuff was always dropping from trees in the forest – bits of bark and sticks dislodged by birds and squirrels, dead insects floating down, loose pine needles blown by the wind. Minnie picked up a nice hefty stick from the trail. She bashed it against the nearest tree and it made a solid satisfying *klunk*. Somewhere in the woods she heard a woodpecker, making its distinctive drumming sound.

'Ah hah!' said Minnie, 'the distant drumming of the yellow-bellied sapsucker.'

'*You're* a yellow-bellied sapsucker!' said Billy.

'No,' said Minnie, '*you're* a yellow-bellied sapsucker!' This familiar exchange never failed to make them laugh.

'*You're* a yellow-bellied sapsucker,' said Billy. 'Is this a trail?'

'Not a hiking trail, no,' said Minnie.

'Mom says I must stick to the trails.'

'Well, it is a trail,' said Minnie. 'It's a game trail. Look, deer prints.' They stopped and examined the small hoof-prints in the soft ground.

'They went that-a-way!' said Billy.

'Ya don't say, Sherlock!' said Minnie. They ran up the trail following the tracks. 'Oh, a flutter of butterflies,' said Minnie and they watched as the butterflies danced around each other, in a cloud of flittering, dipping, twisting white wings. '*Flutter* is the collective noun for butterflies, Billy, like a *swarm* of bees and a *pride* of lions.'

'Mom says if a mountain lion approaches you should stop, stand your ground, make yourself big.'

'Not much hope for you there, Billy-Bug.'

'I'll stand on a rock and roar like a lion!'

'Reckon you could outrun a lion?'

'Yes! Yes, I could!' said Billy with his hands on his hips, feet planted wide like a brave warrior.

'Dan says no lion's been seen since people built cabins here,' said Minnie. 'They've got plenty to eat higher up.'

'Ah, well, good. That's good,' said Billy, heading on up the hill. Minnie bent down, lifted a handful of pine needles and sniffed it.

'Mm, I love this smell. Hey, Billy!'

He stopped and looked back at Minnie who was now kneeling down with one ear to the ground.

'Billy, do this.' Billy did as he was told and knelt down putting his head to the earth. In the deepest voice Minnie could manage she said, 'Stage coach passed by here, with … with four horses.'

'Oh yeah?' said Billy.

'Ask me how I know that,' said Minnie, her head still pressed to the earth.

'How do you know that? Can you hear their hooves galloping away?' asked Billy.

'Nope. It ran over my head!' said Minnie. This made Billy laugh so much he rolled on his back, rocking from side to side holding his belly, cackling like a hyena. Minnie started to tickle him under his arms.

'No! No!' yelled Billy.

'Woah there!' Minnie stopped tickling him.

'Billy! Look! What is that!?' She pointed at the ground. Between them was a hollow in the dark-brown soil where the duff gave way to a muddy path.

'Hey look. There's something in this muddy path away from the duff,' she said.

'What's duff?' asked Billy.

'Oh, Billy. Billy, Billy, Billy. Duff is this layer of old leaves, twigs, bits of bark and pine needles. You know, the brown stuff.'

There was something curious about the shape of the hollow and Minnie crouched down to look more closely. She brushed some leaves out of the impression with her fingers and realised then what it was she was looking at – it was a footprint. It was a footprint of what looked like a human foot, but a human *giant's* foot, because it was so very large. There was a big toe, and four distinct smaller toes. The big toe was about the size an imprint of a small lemon would leave if pressed into the mud. The pinkie toe was slightly spread away from the others like the foot had slipped slightly, and the toes had spread out for extra grip.

'What is that?' Billy asked quietly.

'It is a footprint.' They both peered at it. Minnie

put her foot next to it. It was smaller than a third of the size of the print. 'Wow. It's huge!'

'Minnie? Who made this?' whispered Billy.

'Dan?' suggested Minnie.

'Oh right, Dan.'

'Must be Dan,' said Minnie, 'but I've never really noticed his feet were so big.'

'Let's run back and measure his feet,' suggested Billy.

'Yeah, we should,' said Minnie, and Billy started off down the trail. 'Wait, Billy! Let's see if there's any more!'

They searched the trail. The forest was still. There was not a sound – no birds singing, no bees buzzing. Not a single creature seemed to be stirring. The wind had dropped to nothing and the forest was totally, totally silent. Billy took hold of Minnie's sleeve.

'So quiet,' Minnie said. 'Maybe a storm coming.' They both looked up at the sky visible in patches between the towering pines. It was a clear pale blue and it seemed like the thundercloud across the bay had indeed blown north and not brought its rain to the mountain range.

Minnie carefully stepped up the trail looking at

the ground. About six feet up the trail she pointed to the ground. 'Another one, left foot this time.'

'Minnie, why would Dan walk in here with bare feet when there's pinecones, and roots and ants…?'

'And snakes.' said Minnie.

'I wanna go back now, Minnie.'

'Here's another one. Right foot this time.' Minnie placed a long, thin stick next to the print and broke the end off in line with the big toe.

Musto came running back to them from up the trail. He stopped, looked back the way he came, and sniffed the air, twitching his wet, black nostrils. He took a few steps backwards with his tail between his legs. Minnie noticed this somewhat odd behaviour but decided not to draw Billy's attention to it as that might freak him out even more. Musto moved behind Minnie's legs and she stroked his head.

'Minnie, the hairs on my arms are standing up. That's never happened before.'

'Me neither.' Minnie put a comforting hand on his shoulder. 'We need to mark this spot.'

'Why?' he asked.

'So we can find it again!' she said.

'We don't need to find it again. Let's go!'

Minnie pulled a twig out of the tall grass. It had a V-shaped hook to it and was stripped of its bark.

'Perfect,' she said, and she hung it from a low pine branch near the trail. 'OK. Let's go!'

They ran back down the trail, leaping and bounding over roots and low scrub until they came to the main track down to the cabins. As they slowed to a walk, panting heavily, Minnie passed Billy the water bottle. He took a long slug of water, wiped his mouth on his arm and said, handing it back to her, 'Minnie, did you get the feeling we were being watched?'

'Uh huh,' she answered. 'Still got it.'

'Run!' Billy yelled, and they sprinted down the trail towards the cabins, squealing with a little bit of fear and a lot of excitement.

They didn't stop running until they reached Connie's cabin. Minnie and Billy flopped down on the warm grass by the track, chests heaving, and didn't move until they got their breath back.

'Let's go,' said Minnie. They got to their feet and ran down past the garden and past Minnie's tree to the cabin where Dan was working. Kneeling down and looking under the cabin, they could see just his legs on the other side. They crawled in under the raised floor, and they scrabbled across the dim and dusty space to the wall he was painting. Minnie reached out with the stick in her hand and tried to put it next to his boot to measure it. Just at that moment Dan climbed the ladder, and his foot was out of reach.

'Shoot!' exclaimed Minnie.

'Hello? Where are you, Minnie?' said Dan.

'Oh, under the cabin.'

'Why are you under the cabin?'

'Because I have never been here before.'

'Oh.'

'Yes. And I fully intend to go everywhere!'

Minnie had decided she'd work as a flight attendant while she was training to be a pilot. She thought this would please Dan, who used to be a pilot himself before he met Minnie's mom, and anyway she wanted to see the whole world and flying is a good way to do that. When she was younger she'd wanted to fly transport planes and deliver things to people, like Santa Claus. Now she was older she liked the idea of delivering people to places, to reunite families and friends, in a super-fast jumbo jet.

'It would be more helpful if you dug up some potatoes from the garden for supper,' said Dan, 'There's a fully functional fork!'

'Uh huh,' mumbled Minnie, as she and Billy crawled out from under the cabin, brushing away the clinging spider webs. She raised the stick up towards Dan's boot, but he climbed even further up the ladder with his paint can and brush. She nudged Billy with her elbow and they shot off towards the main cabin.

Dan caught sight of them as they ran between cabins. 'Minnie! Potatoes!'

In the cabin by the front door was a small cupboard with shelves for all their footwear. 'Hold your breath, Billy, or you will die a ghastly death by suffocating intoxication, otherwise known as sneakerissimus-stinky-bumbakissimus.' Minnie opened the door to the cupboard with a flourish and with the stick lifted out one of Dan's sneakers.

'Stinky bumbakissamus! Ha!' Billy laughed as

she put the sneakers on the floor. She put the thin stick next to one of them. The shoe came up to just over half the stick's length.

'Oh,' said Minnie. 'Darn. Now we have a mystery on our hands.' But she had an idea what they might be dealing with and she turned to Billy, wagging the stick at him, and said the word. 'Bigfoot.'

'Sure is,' said Billy. 'But whose foot is it?'

Chapter Four

It was dusk. The sun had sunk behind clouds beyond the hills across the bay and Dan was sitting outside the cabin drinking a beer whilst cleaning his rifle. The water, though a deep blue-green by day, turned black at twilight, with just a few sparkling lights from passing boats in the bay.

There was a silvery-blue glow from the living-room window. Minnie was at the table gazing at the laptop screen. She had a notepad beside her and she scribbled notes in it as she read.

'Isn't it time you turned in?' Dan yelled from outside. 'You've been on that thing for hours.'

'Could be,' she yelled back. 'You tell me, you're the grown-up.'

'It's time to turn in. What you looking at anyway? Homework stuff, I hope!' Minnie shut the laptop.

'Yeah, er, it's the habits of migrating elephants! Fascinating!'

She heard Dan outside repeat the phrase

27

'*migrating elephants*' but she couldn't tell if he didn't believe her or just thought it was a strange thing to study at school.

Minnie pushed the chair back and went outside. As she came out onto the deck Dan sniffed and wiped his nose.

'Hayfever?' she asked. Dan blew his nose with a piece of paper towel, and continued wiping the gun oil off the rifle in his lap.

'Uh huh,' he said, as she sat down on the wooden bench next to his chair. 'Grass pollen. Your mom used to make me drink ginger and garlic tea for it. I did not relish the taste I can tell you that.'

'Dan? Can we do something together tomorrow?'

Her question hung in the air a while, until Dan cleared his throat.

'Hmm. Um … what, like, after school?' asked Dan.

'It's a Saturday tomorrow and besides, Dan, it's first day of summer break.'

'Oh. Right. Really?'

She shook her head, unable to comprehend how Dan could possibly not know it was summer break tomorrow – the most glorious date in the whole calendar, after Minnie's birthday.

'Like, erm, like … like do what?' Dan asked.

Minnie leaned back casually with her hands behind her head and said, 'Oh, you know, go for a hike in the forest?'

'A hike?'

'Yes,' she said. 'And maybe we could do some foraging.'

'Foraging?' Dan asked.

'Mom used to hike in the forest and, you know, forage.'

'Yeah. She did,' said Dan. 'She did.'

'Maybe you could show me where she'd go?'

Dan scratched his bristly beard. 'She'd come back with mushrooms, wild onions, berries. She was always hoping to find some honey,' he said. 'She'd follow bees.' He looked out across the water, and for a few moments was lost in the memory. He smiled. 'Good for hayfever, local honey.'

'And way tastier than ginger and garlic,' said Minnie. 'Let's see what we can find tomorrow.'

'OK,' said Dan.

Minnie climbed into her bed and lay there looking out of her window at the half moon that had just risen. It cast a silvery hue across the starlit sky and the walls of her room.

She soon fell asleep. She dreamed about the day she and Dan had scattered her mother's ashes out in the bay from canoes, while her mom's friends stood on the jetty and watched. Then Dan had paddled off on his own, not looking back. In her dream, when she paddled back there was no one there on the jetty, and she had never felt more alone. And that was how she'd felt on the day, even with all her mom's friends there – completely alone.

While she stood on the jetty looking out across the bay, there came from the highest slopes of the mountain behind her, the loudest, longest *howl*, that echoed and echoed across the water. She woke up. The moon had moved round, and her room was dark, but that howl still echoed in her mind. Minnie climbed out of bed and stood at the window looking up at the mountain silhouetted against a million pinpricks of light in a curtain of night.

Chapter Five

The next morning Minnie was up early and was chomping on some toast and drinking a glass of fruit juice through a straw when Dan came out of the bedroom dressed in his usual jeans and a T-shirt.

'Morning. Why are you up so early on a Saturday?' he asked. 'And first day of summer break?'

'To get ready for our hike.'

'Oh right. Our hike. You still want to go?'

'Er, yes, I still want to go. When I decide to do something, I do it.'

Minnie's mom had always said, 'Minnie if you decide to do something and it feels right in your gut, then do it!' And hiking with Dan back up to that place felt right.

'And how ready are you?' asked Dan as he grabbed the glass coffee jar from the shelf and twisted it open. Minnie scribbled a final note in her little pad and flipped it shut.

'Completely so,' she said.

'OK, well, let me grab some coffee,' he said.

'OK, but…' and with a *thud* Minnie dumped a large red thermos flask on the table, 'make it *to go*.'

The blazing sunshine had warmed the earth and with the heat rose up forest odours of piny resin, flowering sweet-scented clover and earthy mud from the game trails. There was a slight breeze blowing in from the bay shifting the tops of the huge redwoods, pines, cedars and firs. Leaf litter and dust blew down from the trees at an angle and caught the sunlight like a shower of golden flakes falling in slow motion. Dan and Minnie walked up the trail, both carrying small backpacks. Dan carried his rifle.

'Why did you bring your gun, Dan? It's not hunting season.'

'I know.'

'Mountain lion?' she asked. 'Bear?'

'Just habit,' he said. 'Too low down for cat or bear.' They walked on.

'Is it true you can hear pine-cones popping open on a real hot day, Dan?'

'White pines open to disperse the seeds when it's warm and dry, then the cone drops. You can hear a cone drop on dry pine needles if you listen hard.' They stopped and listened.

'Wrong time of year,' said Dan.

'Let's go this way,' said Minnie, stepping off the main trail up the smaller trail she and Billy had taken the previous day. Her feet crunched softly on the leaves and pine needles under foot.

'Some jack pines hold their cones for ten, twenty years, waiting for a fire,' said Dan.

'Won't the fire burn up the cones?' Minnie queried as she threw a pinecone at a tree.

'Forest fires are driven by wind,' Dan said. 'The cone opens in the heat and the wind blows the seeds away, sometimes miles.'

Minnie was looking down at the ground as she walked, and up in the trees. She slowed and stopped by the V-shaped twig she'd left hanging from the branch.

'Fires are scary for animals,' said Dan, 'but they help clear choking underbrush for, you know, fresh healthy growth.'

'Let's take a break,' she said, pulling the backpack off.

'Here?' asked Dan. 'We just got started.'

'Yup, I'm thirsty.'

Dan was looking around warily at the trees, up the trail, all around.

'Let's sit, Dan. Here. Let's sit here.' Minnie sat down right where she was, by the first massive footprint, opening her backpack.

'You sit. I'm fine,' said Dan.

'Come on, Dan.' She patted the ground next to her as she took a swig from her water bottle. He looked at her quizzically. That's when he saw it, right in front of Minnie, inches from her foot. He stared at the massive footprint.

'What…?' He stepped closer. He peered closely. 'That's…'

'Oh, my, what is that, Dan? It looks like a, what, a…?'

He looked up the trail, and around. He then put his boot next to the footprint. The print was *much* bigger than his boot. He crouched down and looked at it *really* closely.

Minnie stood up and moved up the trail. 'Here's another one, Dan.'

He joined her. Together they slowly stepped up the trail scanning the ground for more. 'Here. And look, Dan, this is the right foot again. That's a big stride, huh?'

Dan took his phone out of his pocket. He photographed all the prints, up real close, putting his boot next to them for reference.

'In this one I can see dermal ridges,' said Dan, crouching low to the ground.

'What's dermal ridges?'

'All the little swirls and whorls on your fingers and palm. And creases and lines.' Dan then looked down the trail. 'Just these four. Must have come out of the brush down there, walked up here and cut into the brush up there.'

'So who or what made these footprints, Dan?' *I know*, she thought, *but I need to hear you say it.*

'Dunno,' he said.

'Don't know? You don't know? Bigfoot! A Bigfoot made them!' She stood in front of him and looked him in the eye. 'Bigfoot, also known as Sasquatch, made these footprints, Dan.'

'We don't know that,' he said, still gazing down at the prints. 'Could be fake.'

'Fake? How, Dan? How can they be fake?'

'A guy steps there then raises his foot and steps on his own print again to make it bigger and so, it looks like that.'

'What guy?' she asked.

'Hunter, hiker, logger, boy scout…' he said.

'No. That's not what happened: it's not hunting season, there's no logging here, since the fire there's been no hikers and certainly no boy scouts!' said Minnie.

'You don't know that with absolute certainty,' said Dan.

'Why would someone do that, Dan? Up here? Up this little biddy trail I just found? Huh? Why? On the off-chance that someone would come along and it would blow their mind? You think he's hiding behind a tree now laughing at how he's fooled us? Maybe he's been waiting up here near his phony fake footprints for days, waiting for someone to come along! Yes, yes, that's what happened! Someone faked them! Dan, please!'

She walked on up the trail, then stopped and turned. 'If you're so sure they are fake, why did you take a ton load of photos then? You know they are real and you just can't handle it!' She stomped on up the path, really frustrated.

'Wait, Minnie, wait for me, darn it!'

'Scared of the Bigfoot, Dan?' She kept on walking. 'If they're fake, why are you holding your gun like that?' Dan held his rifle at the ready, finger near the trigger.

'Let me go in front,' he said, passing her.

'Oh, to protect me? From what, Dan? There aren't any Bigfoots up here, are there?'

They hiked on in silence, Dan scanning left and right. 'Don't worry, Dan, they're mostly nocturnal.'

They walked up the trail looking on the forest floor for more prints, but Dan was really twitchy. The slightest sound in the forest like a squirrel chattering or a bird whistling would make him swing the rifle round towards the source of the noise. It was unnerving to Minnie and she said, 'OK, this hike is officially over. Why don't we head back?'

'Why?' he asked.

'Because you keep pointing your gun at things and that is not relaxing!'

Dan looked at her and said, 'I'm perfectly fine to continue looking for an oompah loompah or whatever you think is up here, but if you want to turn back … fine.'

Thunk! A pinecone hit Dan on the shoulder. It dropped to the ground beside them. They looked at the pinecone, looked at each other…

'It came from over there.' Minnie pointed to bushes about twenty yards away.

37

'Must have been a squirrel,' said Dan.

'It wasn't dropped! It was thrown!' Minnie said.

They both stood perfectly still and silent, listening, watching the bushes.

Finally Dan whispered, 'Squirrel. Tree rat. Must've been.' He looked around, his rifle held ready at his hip.

'A squirrel with a bionic right arm,' said Minnie.

'Shush!'

'Why are you shushing me, Dan?'

'I'm trying to listen.' They both stood stock still, listening for any noise, looking for any movement.

'Billy? I know you're over there!' Dan said, staring into the bushes where the pinecone came from.

'Shush!' said Minnie.

'Why are you shushing me?' asked Dan.

'I don't know. I'm scared,' she said. 'You're being too loud…'

'I have this,' he said, as he raised the rifle to his shoulder.

'I feel like we should quietly…' she started to say.

'Retreat. I agree,' said Dan. 'We could start heading back if you want.'

'Fine,' said Minnie.

'Good,' said Dan.

They hurried back down the trail, away from the bushes from where the pinecone was thrown, through the scrubby underbrush, and didn't slacken their pace until they reached the main hiking trail.

'Phew! That was freaky, right, Dan? Having a pinecone thrown at you by an actual Bigfoot! You should count yourself lucky!' Dan ignored her and kept marching down the hill. 'Wow, and those prints, Dan! Pinecones, prints! What a day! Wow! I just realised I talk a lot when I'm frightened!'

'Minnie, there's no such thing as Bigfoot. There's one fuzzy film from the 1960s of a big guy in a monkey suit. That's it.'

'That wasn't a guy in a monkey suit … they proved it can't be.'

'And some Yeti footprints in the snow in Nepal!' he said.

'It was Tibet, Dan, and Native Americans have handed down stories of encounters with giant hairy men in the woods for, like, ever!'

'There's no evidence,' he said.

'Footprints!' she yelled.

'Faked,' he said.

'They've recorded tracks miles long!' she said.
'So?'

'In mud! In winter! With a really long stride length! How did they fake that? When we get back I'll show you. There's video of a three-mile trackway. In the snow, Dan. In the middle of nowhere!' They were in sight of the cabins now.

'There's no scientific proof, Minnie. A body! We need a body!' He said, quite angrily.

'Do the research, Dan, and then we can have a discussion!'

'Oh please!' he said, kicking a small rock off the path as he charged on ahead.

Chapter Six

Minnie and Dan emerged from the trail behind Connie and Billy's cabin. Musto bounded over to them, his feathery yellow tail swooshing, followed by Billy who breathlessly blurted out, 'Did you see…?'

'Bigfoot prints, Billy? No, we did not, as there is no such thing as Bigfoot according to my field guide here.'

Dan eyed Billy suspiciously.

'What have *you* been doing this morning, Billy?' asked Dan.

'Oh, nothing much. Mom's got something for you, Dan,' said Billy.

'Well, that was a lousy hike,' muttered Minnie walking away down the track towards her home.

'I heard that,' said Dan as he walked away towards Connie's cabin.

'What happened?' asked Billy, falling in step with Minnie.

'Come on, I'll tell ya.' They ran down the slope,

but just then the aroma of apple pie, carried by the breeze, hit Minnie. 'Pie!' She stopped as Billy ran on ahead, and following her nose she headed straight back towards Connie's cabin.

Dan and Connie sat on chairs on the deck of the cabin whilst Minnie stood below the deck out of sight and listened in to their conversation. She wanted to hear Dan share with Connie what he thought they'd found.

'Say Connie, has Billy been here this whole time?' asked Dan.

'What, where, here? Yes, why?'

'Oh, no reason. We found something up there,' said Dan.

On the low wooden table between them was a perfect apple pie, with three small ceramic blackbirds sticking their heads through the pastry.

'What are those?' Dan asked.

Standing on the tips of her toes, Minnie peeped over the edge of the deck.

'Bird vents. Like pie chimneys to let the steam out, so I have perfect crusty pastry.'

'Oh, right.'

The smell of the freshly baked apple pie was making Minnie's mouth water. Crouching down, she dumped her backpack and took a gulp from her bottle.

'Dan, before you tell me what you found, I've been meaning to talk about, well … you know it's real important to talk, and, well … it's just you and Minnie down there and…'

'We're doing fine, Connie,' said Dan.

'Are you? She's a twelve-year-old girl who just lost her mom, and she and you…'

'We're OK, Connie.'

'No, darn it, I'm gonna say it. When you met Georgina, you had no notion that within two years she'd be gone and you'd be stuck with her kid.'

'Connie…'

'It's a lot to ask of a man. You and Minnie are clearly not that close. It would be understandable if you wanted to move on. It would, Dan.'

Minnie leant her head against the deck's corner support post, worried now about what she'd hear next, and wishing she wasn't eavesdropping but was with Billy by the shore looking in rock pools, or just lying on the grass in the sun with Musto.

'I do not want to move on,' said Dan. 'I can't.'

Connie looked at him for a few moments.

'Piece of pie? This is for you both, but we could

eat a slice if you liked. It's a fine pie, if I say so myself, with just a dash of cinnamon and ginger in there.'

Minnie heard the cake knife on the plate as Connie cut a piece of pie and continued with, 'We love Minnie. Minnie could live with us…'

'I promised Georgie I would care for Minnie until she's eighteen,' said Dan, 'and old enough to sell this place if she wants to. And I'm gonna do that.'

'Out of a sense of duty or because you love and care for that child?' Hearing all this was excruciating for Minnie and she screwed up her face and softly bumped her head against the post. Connie said, 'She should still be talking to that therapist about her feelings, to help her process her grief and…'

'Minnie decided she didn't need to see the therapist any more,' Dan said firmly.

'She's twelve, Dan.'

Minnie stood on her tiptoes again, her curly hair, forehead and brown eyes partly obscured by the wooden deck rail, thinking she might just have to cough or scream to stop this torture.

'A real smart twelve,' Dan said, as he looked out

at the bay, the islands, the hazy hills on the far side. 'So much like her mom… She knows what she wants and what she likes, and it's not living here with me!'

'Dan! How can you know that? Her mother recently passed and she's trying to deal with that! You two both have to try harder. You are the grown-up, Dan, not her! So…' Connie pulled the plate with the pie towards her and lifted the knife. 'You need to try harder.'

Dan remained silent. As she cut another slice of pie Connie asked, 'So, what did you find in the forest?'

Dan looked back up at the mountain, squinting in the sunlight. He tugged the peak of his cap down to shade his eyes.

'Ah, well, it doesn't matter,' he mumbled.

Minnie couldn't contain herself and yelled, 'It *does* matter!'

Dan stood up. 'Minnie!'

'She heard us, Dan. Every word.'

'I know. I'll go after her,' he said, putting down his plate. 'We found prints, Connie. Footprints.' He held his hands out, palms facing each other, indicating the length of the prints. 'Yay big.'

Connie's forkful of pie hovered an inch from her open mouth.

'Oh. Good,' she said. 'They're back.'

'Where did she go?' Dan ran down the steps. 'Minnie! Wait!'

Minnie had crawled in under Connie's deck and, with tears streaming down her cheeks, she watched Dan run off down the track.

Connie heard Minnie's sniffling. 'Minnie?' Minnie crawled out from under the deck, wiping the tears and snot away with the sleeve of her shirt.

'Oh Minnie, come here.' Connie enveloped the sobbing girl in her arms. The sweet woody smell of the frankincense resin that she always burned in the cabin, clinging to the wool of the soft cashmere cardigan, took Minnie instantly back to the small wooden church in town where they'd had the memorial service for her mother. She realised in that instant that the two smells were the same – the church and Connie's cabin.

She sobbed without stint, her whole body heaving with despair. 'Let it out, darling girl, let it out,' Connie whispered as she held her tight. And she did. She let it out. As the waves of anguish slowly began to recede, Minnie allowed herself to believe that she was being comforted by an actual Angel of Kindness, because Connie was surely the second-kindest person she'd ever known.

'I don't want to live here anymore, Connie!'

'Come now, Minnie darlin', this is your home. You were born here.'

'Everywhere reminds me of Mom!'

'Good! Me too!' said Connie.

'Dan doesn't even like me!'

'He loves you, Minnie; he just isn't ready to show it yet. He's grieving too!' Connie sat her down and poured her a glass of lemonade. 'Dan says you found Sasquatch prints in the forest. That's exciting! They used to be here long ago, or so I'm told.'

'They don't want us here neither! One threw a pinecone at Dan!'

'Really?'

'Yeah. Don't you see? It's a sign. A sign we should leave! All of us, but especially me.'

'Where would you go?' asked Connie. 'Your mom's folks in South Bend, Indiana? Surely not! I won't allow it.'

'I can go there if I want!' insisted Minnie. 'I don't want to be here!'

'This place would not be worth living in with you gone, Minnie. You are the life and soul of this little corner of the world! You are! You have your mother's indomitable spirit and we need you here! Those Bigfoots, or Sasquatches as I prefer to call them, up there in the forest, hold ancient wisdom and they recognise kindred souls. Things happen for a reason.' She took both Minnie's hands in hers. 'Now let's together breathe deeply this pure beautiful air, from the sea and from the forest.' Connie closed her eyes. 'You'll feel better. Come on, breathe with me, *in* two three four, and *out* two three four five, *in* two three four five six, *out* two three four five six seven…'

And, though Minnie tried to breathe in time with Connie, she couldn't because the way Connie was squeezing her eyes shut made her face look funny, and Minnie couldn't help laughing, and then Connie started laughing with her. After the crying, the laughter made her nose run again, and she blew it on a piece of paper towel, and helped herself to a piece of pie.

Later, Dan was on the deck watching the sun go down behind the far-off hazy grey hills, drinking beer from a bottle. The tide was out and the aromas of the shoreline reached the cabin. The smell of salty, wet, seaweed-covered rocks, and damp, muddy sand mingled with the sharp pine resin from the trees that hugged the rocky shoreline on both sides of the cabin clearing. Minnie was inside, curled up in a corner of the sofa with the laptop on her knees. She looked at Dan, his head just visible outside, framed by the golden glow of the sunset lighting the window. She put the laptop on the table and came out on to the deck.

'Night, Dan.'

'You turning in?' he asked.

'Yup.'

'Want another piece of pie, Minnie?'

'Just brushed my teeth.'

'Minnie?'

'Yes?'

'You OK?'

'Uh huh.'

'Listen, I'm sorry about earlier. I should … and … I will, well, I will try … harder.'

'Thanks.' She turned to go. 'Me too.'

And she went back inside the cabin. A few moments later Dan got up and went inside too. At the table he tapped on the laptop keyboard and the screen lit up. Minnie peeped through the gap she'd left in the doorway to her bedroom and saw him sit down and look at the page she had intentionally left open on the laptop. She smiled and closed the door quietly.

Chapter Seven

It was a shiny, sunny Sunday morning and Minnie came out of her room dressed and ready for the day. Dan was on the computer. He looked up and said, 'Oh. Hi.' It was unusual for Dan to be on the computer at this hour of the day. Most mornings when Minnie emerged from her room he'd already be outside working.

'You been up all night?' she asked.

'Nope. Just got up.'

'What ya lookin' at?' she asked.

Dan closed the laptop as he answered, 'Oh, nothin' much. Migrating elephants. Want to go for a hike with me,' Dan said as he pulled on his coat, 'to see what we can see?'

Minnie looked at him and took a bite of her apple. She smiled. 'OK.'

'But later,' said Dan. 'I have to service the wind turbine now and…'

'So what am I going to do all day? Can't we go hiking now? The turbine's not going anywhere.'

'No, Minnie. In fact, I'd appreciate some help. Like maybe do some weeding in the garden or dig the potatoes?'

So as Dan got set to climb up to the wind turbine behind the cabin, Minnie wandered over to her mother's vegetable garden, yanked the fork out of the ground and wondered what to do with it.

Minnie spent the rest of the morning in the garden. The small vegetable plot had been her mother's pride and joy. All manner of vegetables and fruit had thrived there under her care, but since she became ill it had grown untidy. The caneberry bushes had spread their spiky canes in to the other beds and grasses and weeds had been allowed to spread and choke the plants.

Though she had seen Dan tackle weeds from time to time, he clearly didn't enjoy working in what had been her mother's special place, and would quickly move on to do other chores.

A lot of the morning Minnie just lay on the grassy paths between the beds watching creepy crawlies or peering inside flowers at the beautiful shapes inside the petals. She could remember from school the words 'stamen, carpel and sepal' referring to parts of a flower but she couldn't remember which was which. She grazed on juicy red tomatoes, peppery nasturtium leaves and sweet black caneberries. Reluctantly, and only because she was becoming really bored, she picked up the fork.

The soil was a very dark brown and heavy, and her arms soon began to ache. She lobbed the potatoes she dug up on to the path, each a yellowy nugget still dusted with the life-giving dark soil they'd fed off. Every worm she unearthed she collected up and moved to a safe spot where they wouldn't be sliced by her fork.

After she'd dug enough potatoes she moved over to what smelt like the onion patch, but she couldn't see any onions. She trod on something hard. It was a small wooden peg. She picked it up and rubbed the soil off it. One side was neatly carved flat with her mother's handwriting on it. It read *'Purple Stripe Garlic. Great sliced on a burger – see recipe 6'.* Minnie searched for other pegs. She found two and suspected there were more hidden in the overgrown beds.

Each peg described the plant and what to do with it. *'Parano Carrots – great juiced or in cake – see recipe 11'* and *'Cherokee Purple Tomato – see recipe 9'*. This thrilled her, and she immediately abandoned the digging, tossed the fork away and ran back to the cabin.

Up on the kitchen shelves were various recipe books, none of which Minnie had ever looked at, but among them she found what she was looking for. It was was a red ring binder. There, in her mother's handwriting, were recipes, some with a laminated photo pulled from a magazine to show what it should look like, and each clearly numbered.

There were twenty recipes. Minnie pored over the words, hearing her mother's voice in her head as she read. 'Here's what you do next – mix the chopped and fried wild onion with the breadcrumbs, the lean minced beef, the egg and the handful of Parmesan cheese by scrunching them together in your (washed) hands…'

'Hey, Minnie! You ready for that hike?' Dan called from outside.

54

A short while later Minnie and Dan were walking up the track towards Connie's cabin. 'You hear the wolves last night?' asked Dan.

'No. Sure they were wolves?' asked Minnie.

'Yes, I am. The wolf population north and over the mountain has just gone like, boo koo,' said Dan.

'Boo koo?' she asked.

'Yeah. It's French for many. They eat a lot of meat. I hear they been killing the hell out of the big game.'

'And with the fire on the other side…' began Minnie.

'Yeah, they've spread over this side. The one I heard was way north of here, but still.'

'Billy!' yelled Minnie.

'Don't yell like that. Knock on the door,' said Dan, 'you know, like a normal person.'

'I always yell. For me that's normal.' Billy appeared at the screen door and Musto bundled out behind him, ever pleased to have visitors.

'Billy-Bug, you wanna come? We're going up to you-know-where.'

'Oh, are you? Er, no thanks. I've got a math project to start, well, to finish,' said Billy. 'Well, I haven't started it, but I need to finish it.'

'Math project?' asked Minnie.

'Uh huh. Math. Big summer project,' said Billy. 'I like math.'

'Math project my foot!' said Minnie, stomping her foot on the deck.

'Summer math project,' mumbled Billy.

'OK if we take Musto?' asked Dan.

'Please take Musto with you,' said Billy. 'He's bored.' Musto was wagging his tail so much his whole body bent in the middle, one way then the other.

'Thanks,' said Dan.

Minnie was giving Billy, her one and only playmate and very best friend, the 'old skunk-eye'. Billy, knowing her so well, said, 'I hate to disappoint, but...'

'Well, ya did,' said Minnie and she headed up the track.

'See ya later,' said Dan. 'Let's go, Musto!'

They walked quickly up the trail, with Musto running on ahead. The dog knew to peel off the hiking trail and follow the path they'd made through the brush to the footprints. Minnie and Dan followed Musto, striding up the meandering path beneath the pines and soon the three of them stood together looking down at the prints. 'Shouldn't we cast them?' asked Minnie.

'But they're on a slope,' said Dan. 'Wouldn't the plaster just flow out one end?'

'Oh yeah. Unless we built like, a box around them.'

'Good idea,' said Dan as he knelt, taking a tape measure out of his pocket.

'Oh, so you know about casting plaster prints of Bigfoots now, Dan?'

'*Suspected* Bigfoots. I might have read something about it,' he said with a wry smile. 'And we have seventeen inches. Wow.'

'Ha! Hey, maybe we'll find some more on a flat part of the trail. Come on, Dan.' They continued on their way. After about twenty minutes of following game trails up the slope they rounded a bend and it opened on to a small sloping meadow with about thirty pale, elegant aspen trees grouped near the centre. Beyond them the forest continued and it was darker and even denser than the part they'd just walked through. They strolled through the stand of aspens, their small flat leaves trembling in the breeze. Minnie suddenly stopped dead in her tracks. 'Dan. Are you seeing what I'm seeing?'

'What are you seeing?' asked Dan.

'An X.'

'What? Where?'

'Don't you see it? There, Dan.' Dan peered into the shade of the tree line. And then he saw it. The slim trunks of two pine trees had together somehow formed a perfectly symmetrical X.

'Nice.'

'Nice? Nice, Dan? That marks the beginning. Follow me.'

Musto had already run on ahead into the trees and they could hear him crashing through the underbrush. 'Musto!' yelled Minnie. 'He must be chasing a squirrel.'

They moved through the stand of white aspens. Minnie exclaimed, 'Bender!'

'Excuse me?' said Dan.

Minnie had her notepad open. 'Look. A bent-over tree or branch making a pinned arch, to indicate the way to go. Sometimes, but not always indicating the way to go. But here it does because … look!'

She pointed in the direction the bent tree was pointing and it was right *at* the X in the tree line. 'According to my research, as we go futher up the mountain we will see more and more of these, Dan. Bender! Check!'

Dan inspected the slim white-trunked aspen. The tip of the tree seemed to have been bent over and another heavy dead branch had been placed on the thin end to keep it touching the ground. 'A person could have done that,' he said.

'A person *could* have done that,' said Minnie, 'but why?'

They walked towards the X. Standing underneath the two crossed pine trees Minnie said, 'Dan, if we go straight on up from here I guarantee there will be more Xs and tree structures. Are you ready for this?'

'What is that smell?' Dan said, looking down at the ground. 'Oh. We're standing on wild onion.' He bent down and pulled up a green leaf, bit into it and walked over to the base of the trunk of one of the trees in the X.

'This is just storm damage, and they've somehow fallen across each other and...'

'What is it?' asked Minnie.

'There's no root ball. No roots on it.' He walked over to the other tree in the X. 'And they haven't been cut. They've broken in a storm maybe and then, somehow...'

'Yes?' said Minnie.

'Somehow ended up here, in this … this X.'

'See Dan, how the bark and the branches have all been stripped off,' said Minnie, 'Would or could men have done this, Dan?'

'Erm… Yes, by lifting them with ropes and pulleys.'

'But, again, why? What you don't yet get, Dan, is that the same tree structures show up all over North America, wherever there have been sightings of Bigfoots. I expect to see the following…'

It was nearing evening now and under the dense shaded canopy of pine branches and cedars her notes were harder to read. She coughed to clear her throat then read out loud, 'Xs, teepees, benders, leaners, tridents, breaks, blinds, glyphs and wallows. Not taking notes, Dan? OK. These are terms used by field researchers like me to name all the different structures that Sasquatches make.'

'I don't need to takes notes. I got this.' Dan snapped a photo of Minnie, standing under the X, with his phone. She smiled as he took the picture. Dan looked up at the X and then past Minnie into the dense brush and trees behind her. He called out, 'Musto! Where is that dog?'

Just then Minnie felt a kind of fizzing excitement in her chest, a feeling like being full of light, full of happy energy, and she couldn't stop grinning and she couldn't stop tears coming to her eyes. It felt like her mother was with her, right now in this most beautiful forest, the one that Minnie would always return to from wherever her spirit took her on her life journey. She felt as if the steps she was taking now, with the man who had made her mother the happiest she had ever seen her, were the most important steps she had ever taken in her twelve years on this planet. And she somehow knew that whatever was waiting for her further up this mountain, maybe today or another day soon, was going to teach her and Dan things that would affect their lives in a very deep way.

Then something flew past her head.

'*What was that*?' she screeched.

'What?' said Dan, quickly ducking his head.

'Oh, hi crow,' said Minnie with relief. It was a sleek black crow, its feathers shining in the low shafts of evening light. 'I thought it was another pinecone!'

'Me too!' said Dan.

The crow had landed on a branch nearby and was

looking at them both. It tilted its head this way and that, its beady yellow eyes still bright in the looming shadows as twilight closed in, wrapping the forest in a darkening blanket. The crow flew up to a higher branch and its *caw caw*, echoed through the trees.

'Musto!' Dan called again. Soon the yellow coat of the dog could be seen as he galloped through the trees towards them. 'Let's go.' Musto ran up to them, wagging his tail joyously.

'What you found up there, boy? You been making new friends?' said Minnie. 'Eeuw, Musto. You stink!'

'Musky Musto! What is that stink?' said Dan as he scanned the dense trees the dog just came from.

'Listen,' said Minnie. 'It's all gone very quiet.' And it had – no birdsong, no buzzing, no squirrel chatter, no wind in the trees.

Just then a loud *CLACK!* rang out through the forest.

'Yes!' said Minnie, referring to her notepad, 'Rock clacking. Cool!' Dan was scanning the trees, standing perfectly still, listening.

CLACK! CLACK!

'They want us to leave,' said Minnie.

'Ha! Right!' said Dan.

'Oh, I suppose you think that's Billy and Connie yanking your chain, huh? They're out there smashing rocks together, are they?'

Minnie could sense that Dan was uncomfortable. Though she'd have liked to go higher up the mountain she was content to turn back now, if that's what the Sasquatches wanted, now that they'd found the big X and they'd heard *rock clacking*! 'You want to go back, Dan?'

'No! Why? We're having a nice hike!' Just then there was a series of quick loud *cracks* followed by a noise like splintering, breaking wood, then a whooshing and then a really loud *CRASH!* And a *WHUMP!*

Dan just stood open-mouthed staring up the slope. 'We should go.'

They quickly turned to hike back down the trail.

'What *was* that?' asked Dan.

'They pushed a tree down, Dan! They pushed a tree down!'

'Run!' he yelled.

'Sorry, sorry, we're going, we're going,' called out Minnie, grabbing Musto by the collar and dragging him away from the tree line. The crow swooped down past them and landed on a branch high in a pine. It kept flitting from tree to tree, keeping up with them.

Dan said, 'It's staying with us. That's....'

'Weird,' said Minnie. 'Wow! Rock clacking *and* a tree pushed over! We are *so* lucky, Dan.'

Dan stopped, turned, and looked back up the trail with his rifle raised to his shoulder. He scanned the trees and listened.

'So, what do you think that was? Huh? Huh, Dan?'

'Shush! I'm listening.' After a few moments he said, 'It was nothing. A tree fell in the woods.'

'Oh Dan. Dan, Dan, Dan...'

'Let's go,' he said.

'You don't wanna talk about it?' asked Minnie.

'Nope.' And Dan just kept right on walking, occasionally glancing back up and around at the trees. The whole way down the mountain the crow cawed from a high branch and then flew silently on to its next vantage point, and cawed again, keeping with them until they left the forest.

They finally emerged into the cabin clearing at twilight. In the dimness the cabins were barely visible and the waters of the bay had turned a dark, dark grey.

Chapter Eight

The next morning Connie, Billy, Musto, Dan and Minnie were sitting on the small wooden floating jetty that jutted out in to the bay. It was designed so that it rose and fell with the water, resting on pontoon posts when the tide was out. Minnie looked out at the bay and thought of the many times she and her mom had fished off the end of the jetty when the tide was in. They'd catch lake trout, brown trout and sometimes dolly vardens – beautiful silver fish with grey and pink spots down their flanks. Trout was her favourite to eat. When the tide was out they'd gather the shiny mussels that grew tightly packed in clusters, like dozens of black, grey and brown oval jewels, on the rocks and posts under the jetty and eat those with the trout.

As the tide slowly receded, lengths of slimy greeny-brown seaweed were left draped over the rocks along the shoreline and Minnie gazed, mesmerised by the thousands of black flies dancing and buzzing in clouds above them.

There were two small green rowboats moored at the jetty. Billy climbed down and sat in one of them. They were drinking lemonade poured from a large glass jug packed with lemon wedges and mint.

'The crow is a sentinel,' said Minnie.

'A what?' asked Billy.

'A sentinel. It reports back to the Bigfoots. They're friends. They cooperate. We could learn a lot from them.'

'How do you know all this, Minnie?' asked Connie.

'How do you think?'

'Oh. Right. Internet. Well, that's why they called it Howler Mountain. Used to hear howling, yowling, screeching and yelling like you wouldn't believe. And not from wolves! A bigger, louder, resonating sound like a lion or an elephant. A bellowing bass growl that rolls and rises and echoes through the night.'

'Er, thanks, Mom.' said Billy.

Connie continued, 'The tribal elders say the Sasquatch used to be down here. Right here. Living by the shore. They'd feed on the mussels, limpets, seaweed. They were here even before the tribes came.'

'Down here?' asked Billy.

'Yup, in the old days. Cos this here, it's a tidal inlet so, you know, it's all sea water.'

'We know, Mom,' said Billy.

'So there's all manner of life here. Clams, crabs, oysters, snails, sea urchins, mussels. Even better on the other side, on the island there, so much protein just sitting there at low tide. That's why we say, "When the tide is out, the table is laid!"'

'Good one,' said Billy.

Connie smiled. 'But when people moved in here the Sasquatches, they moved up the mountain. Then when people started logging up there, the Sasquatches they gave up and moved on over to the north side there. Didn't like the noise we made.'

'And didn't like having their trees cut down, I'll bet,' said Minnie.

'Yes, I'll bet,' said Billy in agreement.

Minnie pointed up the mountain at the pale grey cloud of smoke. 'But the fire... So they've moved back on this side again?'

'Could be,' said Connie.

'Oh please! We don't know that,' said Dan. 'Connie, you can't be filling their heads with this stuff!'

Connie protested, 'But Dan...'

'But no one's going into that forest,' said Dan. 'Not without me and a gun.'

'But Dan, you don't believe in Bigfoots. Or have you changed your mind?' asked Minnie.

'Wolves,' said Dan.

'Bigfoot ain't dangerous,' said Connie. 'They want nothin' to do with us unless we start bothering them.'

'You're a dreamer, Minnie,' said Dan, 'and dreaming gets you into trouble.'

'I'd rather be a dreamer than a scaredy-cat,' she replied.

'I ain't no scaredy-cat!' yelled Billy, standing up in the boat so quickly it started to wobble under him, so he sat straight back down again. 'I have a math project!'

'I'm not talking about you, Billy. And my mom was a dreamer! She dreamed she'd have a cabin by the water and she got six of them! Seems you've got a lot to thank dreamers for, Dan!'

'Minnie! Hush!' said Connie, standing up.

'I have work to do,' Dan said, getting to his feet. He walked off the jetty and headed up towards the rocky outcrop where the wind turbine stood.

Connie crouched down next to Minnie and said, 'I think you need to apologise to Dan.'

Minnie pushed her hair back and looked into the distance. She felt bad. She stood up to go but Connie took her by the shoulders, looked her in the eyes, and said, 'You two have to work out your differences. He loved your mom too, Minnie. That is the important thing, the thing you have in common. Use it. Use it to help each other.'

Minnie put her arms round Connie and hugged her, and Minnie cried again, and Connie held her again.

Billy sat alone in the rowboat tied to the floating jetty, looking up at his best friend and a tear rolled down his cheek and plopped on to the peeling green boards in the bottom of the boat.

Chapter Nine

Dan was up the ladder working on the wind turbine up on the rocky outcrop, when Minnie walked up the grass path to the cabin. He yelled down to her. 'Hey, Minnie!'

She feared they were going to 'have a talk', which coming from Dan would be so hugely unusual that it would probably unbalance the whole of her universe, and vex her even more. She was still quite annoyed at being called a 'dreamer', like it was a bad thing to be. She hesitated before slowing and stopping and turned to look up at him.

He yelled over to her, 'You OK to stay at Connie's tonight? I'm going into town later.'

After her mother died Dan would sometimes take the truck and drive into town, and sometimes wouldn't reappear until morning. Minnie guessed he drank too much in the bar and slept it off in the truck. On those occasions she would stay with Connie and Billy, and Musto always slept curled up with her, which she loved.

'Sure. Yeah. Fine,' she yelled. She knew this would have been the perfect time to say something to Dan like, *I'm sorry for what I said*, but she didn't and she walked on up to the cabin.

She didn't want to talk to anyone, not even to Billy and Connie and she didn't much want to stay with them that night.

She leant out over the edge of the deck so she could see up to Connie and Billy's cabin, and waited until she saw Connie disappear inside, leaving Billy alone. Then she rushed inside, into the bathroom and climbed out of the small back window.

She let herself hang down holding on to the windowsill, then dropped to the dusty track. She sprinted up the track and breathlessly flopped down next to Billy on the deck.

'Hey Billy-Bug. Can I borrow Musto for the night? I want to persuade Dan we should get a dog.'

'You're getting a dog? That would be great. Musto needs someone to play with and I'm usually way too busy to do that.'

'Yeah, what with your summer math project and all.'

'Yeah, so I'll go get him. Musto!'

71

'Or I can come get him later,' suggested Minnie.
'No. Take him now. He's bored. Musto!'

That afternoon Minnie was digging in the vegetable garden and Musto was helping by digging up slugs and snails and crunching them in his mouth.

'Hey, don't just kill 'em for fun.'

Leaning on her fork, Minnie looked up at the forest and for a few moments she listened, straining her ears as her eyes searched the shadows for movement.

'You up there, mister Bigfoot?'

Birds chirruped and whistled close by and squirrels somewhere chattered. The wind gently tapped high branches together. Satisfied, she plunged her fork in the soil.

She was on the other side of the cabin from where Dan was. She felt more comfortable with some distance between them and she thought that by digging up potatoes without being asked she might help the situation. She was dropping them into a green trug, when she heard the loud *clunk* of a door and the engine of Dan's truck start up.

She watched him drive away through the trees down the track that hugged the shoreline, the only route to the nearest town, which was about a twenty-minute drive away.

In the next bed were sad and untidy tomato plants offering a few tiny red jewels, which Minnie popped into her mouth. They were sweet and juicy and she hunted for more and spied another wooden peg half hidden by a tangle of leaves and hairy green stems. She lifted the name peg and scraped the mud off it. This one had more writing on it than the others she'd found before – *'Hi Minnie! This is called Raven Zucchini! – see recipe 10 (Dan's favourite!)'*

This took her breath away. Her mom had left her a direct message in the vegetable garden! Suddenly Minnie knew what she had to do.

'Musto! Let's go!'

In her bedroom Minnie turned the pages of the folder until she found recipe 10. It was Zucchini Tomato Casserole and she looked down the list of ingredients.

'How hard can this be, Musto? It's just zucchini, tomato, garlic, parsley, onions, lemon, salt, pepper and chilli powder!' She jumped off the bed and ran into the kitchen followed by Musto.

'Right. Dan won't be back till tomorrow which gives me plenty of time to start over if I mess this up.' She opened the cupboard door.

'I see parsley, salt … um … is that chilli powder?' She flipped over the page and read aloud her mom's instructions. 'Minnie, if you ever want to do something nice for Dan, and I'm sure you will eventually, this is quick and easy and he loves it! We should have tomatoes and garlic and zucchini in the garden. If you're not growing any onion you could forage some from the forest. It looks like this. I love you!'

There was a beautifully drawn, coloured sketch of a slim-leaved plant with small star-shaped white flowers and a small white bulb. 'Musto! I know where there's wild onions! I do! Indeed I do!'

She rolled off her bed and started pulling on her hiking boots and gathering things – a coat, two bottles of water, her notepad and a pencil, which she pushed into her backpack, along with a huge chunk of Connie's apple pie, which she wrapped in foil.

'OK, Musto. Let's go get some onions.' She hitched the pack on to her shoulder and she and Musto left the cabin. Minnie felt happy. It was almost like she and her mom were doing something together in making a special meal for Dan.

She leapt off the wooden steps yelling, 'Last one to the trail is a rotten oyster!' She and Musto raced past the vegetable garden.

Chapter Ten

The big footprints on the trail had been walked on by deer and other creatures. Leaves and pine needles had collected in them. She bent down and brushed away some of the leaves. Minnie looked up at the trees towering above the trail, the branches high above her. Only a glimpse of the sky was visible through the swaying dark foliage. She hoped the crow wouldn't show up. She didn't want the crow reporting back to the Bigfoots that she was there. She was just going to pick some wild onions and that was all – a quick hike up and a quick hike down.

'Right, Musto? Just some wild onions and we'll be outta here.'

Minnie reckoned they probably knew she was there anyway, or they would do by the time she got up to the Aspen Grove and the Giant X in the trees. They would have heard her or smelt her or just would have sensed her presence in the forest by then. The forest was their home and they would know every inch of it and its sounds and smells and its animal inhabitants – every single one of them.

Minnie knew she should be frightened to be alone in the forest where there were wild animals – not just busy little squirrels and inquisitive crows, but potentially mountain lions, moose and bear. She knew Dan would not be happy at all if he thought she was here alone, but when he tasted her zucchini and tomato casserole all would surely be forgiven.

She didn't feel alone at all; she had Musto, yes, but also she felt her mother was with her, not exactly walking along beside her, but kind of hanging around somehow, in the trees and the wind and the sunbeams, keeping her safe and guiding her.

There were only the four footprints in the mud as before, but she searched the game trail for more, looking either side of the trail between the bushes and on any patch of mud she could find. She found an indentation, not much bigger than her fist and she guessed it was a deer print.

About twenty minutes later she and Musto came out on to the gently sloping meadow where the aspens grew. She could see where she and Dan had walked and followed the impressions they had left in the knee-high grass to the bent-over sapling, still pinned to the ground by the heavy broken limb. Minnie touched the smooth pale grey bark warmed by the sun and rubbed her flat palms on it.

Minnie looked up the slope to the giant symmetrical X just within the tree line marking the start of the denser, darker forest. She and Musto slowly approached. They stood beneath it.

She looked around. 'Onions,' she said as she crouched down. The pale green plants were giving off a distinctive woody, oniony scent. She gently pulled at a plant, the soft earth giving up the neat white bulb. She pulled two more and put them in her backpack. She closed her eyes and listened and breathed in deeply and felt the forest.

'This way, Musto.' She pointed the way ahead and they ran together under the X and up the trail.

Minnie had to step over logs, tree trunks and deadfall branches that had dropped from above but there was still a visible game trail to follow. Musto ran ahead of her. She watched him as he disappeared behind a stand of firs and then she realised she was looking at *another* giant X – two tree trunks both stripped of their bark, crossed to form another perfectly symmetrical X.

'Yes!' said Minnie. She ran on, then stopped. Just off the trail to one side was a slim tree that had been broken, pulled over at the break, and left pointing in the direction of the trail. She reckoned if she sat on Dan's shoulders she could maybe touch the break. She flipped open her notebook. 'Another giant X and a breaker. Check!' She walked on.

She caught up with Musto. She found him standing on his back legs with his front legs up against a tree. He was looking up into its branches. 'What is it, Musto?' A squirrel scurried along a branch, jumped to a nearby pine and hurried round to the far side of the trunk. 'Oh, a squirrel!' The squirrel reappeared on the other side of the trunk chattering at them. 'Hey, squirrel.'

Just then the black crow arrived and landed on a branch of the same pine tree. 'Oh great, it's you Caw-Caw. You gonna tell on me? Keeping an eye on me, are you?' The crow cawed once, flapped its wings and flew away in the direction of the mountain, up and up towards the summit.

Ahead on the trail a broken tree limb stripped

79

of its bark had been carefully leant up against a redwood tree. Next to the big stick was a smaller one about a foot long. 'Leaner and baby leaner. Check!' She said, making a check mark in her notebook.

'Musto, here boy, keep close,' she whispered to the dog. And they walked on up the trail.

'Oh my goodness!' Minnie put a hand to her mouth in astonishment as straight ahead of her in an open clearing bordered by a ring of giant redwoods was a structure made of straight tree trunks, all stripped of their bark, all leaning together to a high-up point. 'Teepee, Musto. That, we call a teepee. Bigfoots don't live in them, but they must mean something to them.'

But Musto wasn't looking at her; he was looking over at the tree line. He'd seen something. Minnie stepped into the clearing, approached the 'teepee' and looked closely at the bottoms of the tree trunks.

'Broken. None of them cut with a saw.' She looked up. 'Musto?' Musto was not where he was a second ago. Then she heard him bark, just once, somewhere off in the trees.

Minnie headed for the tree line and ran past the

redwoods into the forest. 'Musto!' Where are you?' She stopped because she couldn't go any further.

Ahead of her was a tangled pile of broken branches, some with fresh green pine needles still on them. There were long, straight pine limbs stacked one on top of the other, kind of like a fence. It was too high for her to climb over.

Minnie looked in her notepad. 'Ah hah! This is a blind,' she said. 'A hunting blind to hide behind and wait for unsuspecting deer. But it's kinda like a giant nest!' Musto barked again. She ran around the 'blind'. She was looking at a tangled mass of dark brush, more tree trunks, more bushes, more tangle, more shapes, and shadows.

There was no wind, no movement, no sound, just her heavy breathing. And the only movement was from Musto who was agitatedly pacing back and forth, while looking at one particular spot in the undergrowth between the trees. Then Musto did a curious thing – he stood absolutely still, like a statue. His whole body seemed to quiver, his fur vibrating like he was shivering. Then Musto slowly walked into a small gap in the pile of stacked pine trunks and disappeared into the dense underbrush beyond it.

Minnie was in a daze. She just stood there, staring at the place she'd last set eyes on Musto for what seemed to her like ages. She heard a clear solid *knock!* It was the distinct sound of wood on wood. She put her pack down and stood still listening to the forest. She took a deep breath in and slowly, slowly breathed out.

She opened the notepad. Further away and fainter she heard another answering wood knock. She dropped her pencil. The hairs on her forearms stood up, goosebumps pimpled her skin and Minnie gazed at her arms and rubbed them briskly with her hands.

'Musto! Here! Here boy!' But she couldn't get through the gap Musto had gone through. She had to fight her way through a pile of loose boughs ripped from trees. She found a gap in the brush and followed the trail. She couldn't see Musto's paw prints. There was no mud, only leaf litter and matted, knotty grass.

Far ahead she heard a distant barking, just two 'woofs'. She looked up at the sky and realised the light was beginning to fade. She couldn't leave Musto. She had to find him.

She walked and walked, calling for Musto. The

underbrush gave way to a stone and boulder-strewn path. She came to what she realised was the top of a ridge. The ground sloped down to a ravine with a tumble of grey rocks along the bottom. In the woods on the other side of the ravine she heard barking. It was the same excited barking Musto had made when he'd found a grass snake under one of the cabins; he had picked it up in his teeth and thrown it around until Dan grabbed it off him and ended its torment.

She began scrambling down the steep slope. Loose rocks dislodged no matter how slowly and carefully she climbed. She slipped as a flat rock skidded away from under her boot. She tumbled down the ravine. Her world went black.

Chapter Eleven

Minnie woke to an aching in her head. She was lying on her side on a pile of moss and leaves. As she breathed out a large torn leaf that was stuck under her cheek in front of her nose fluttered as she exhaled, like the whirring of a dragonfly's wings.

She started to pull herself up but there was a pain in her right hand. It was cut under the little finger and oozed blood. Touching her head with her left hand, she could feel a bump and it was wet with blood from a small gash. She wasn't at the bottom of the ravine. She wasn't in the ravine at all, and she was not on the ridge where she had been. To her astonishment she realised she was on top of the wooded ridge on the other side of the ravine from where she'd been.

Minnie realised she must have blacked out for a while as it was much darker now. She looked up at the sky. It would very soon be night.

A chill spread through her body. Her mouth was

dry. Pulling off her backpack, she yanked one of the bottles out and drank from it. She went through the side pockets and in one of them was a small pack of wipes. Her mom must have shoved them in there ages ago. Minnie cleaned the cut on her hand as best she could. Then she sat holding a wipe to her cut head. She looked around. 'Musto!'

For the first time she was afraid. The forest was silent – it was the transition time between daytime creatures and night-time creatures. No wind rustled the twilight treetops, no birds called.

Minnie knew trying to find her way back in the dark would be dangerous and she might walk further in the wrong direction. She wasn't sure she'd be able to get down the ravine safely anyway, and she really didn't want to leave Musto in the woods on his own.

'Mom? What should I do?' She waited for an answer to come to her. She tugged her green jacket out of her pack and pulled it on. She found talking to her mom was a comfort.

'Yes, Mom, I must hunker down somewhere and keep warm, and in the morning walk back and tell Connie I have lost her dog and we'll get a search party with professional trackers organised, and we'll come up here and find Musto, and all will be well once more.'

She walked a little way into the trees where the ground flattened out. In the twilight she could vaguely make out what she was treading on, mostly pine needles and soft, dry leaf litter.

'Darn it. If I smoked I'd have a lighter. Or matches for a fire. Just kidding, Mom. I'm never gonna smoke. I wonder how cold it will get.' There was a fir tree whose lower branches arched low to the ground. Minnie got on her hands and knees and crawled under the boughs. It was even darker inside but felt safe and enclosed. She stretched her legs and began shoving the pine needles out with her booted feet, pushing small piles towards the low hanging branches, digging herself a bowl to curl up in.

Scrabbling in her pack she pulled out the apple pie in tin foil. She sat against the trunk of the tree and ate half of it. She hoped Billy wouldn't start missing Musto and head over to her cabin to look for them. Most likely no one would notice they were gone until Dan came back in the morning and Minnie planned to be home before that happened. Until then she was very much alone.

Just then she heard some rustling in the underbrush outside her small dark den. Something was coming towards her, moving closer and closer.

She heard sniffing, snuffling and panting. In her mind she ran through some animals it could be – porcupine, raccoon, weasel. Then she remembered mountain lions, coyotes, and…

Musto! He pushed his way in through the branches and she grabbed him. 'Oh Musto! Musto! Thank you!'

She curled up with her arms round Musto who licked away the tears on her cheeks and, though a long dark night was just beginning, things weren't nearly so bad now they were together.

KAAYII

Chapter One

High, high, high up in a pine tree on the ridge near the summit of the mountain sat the young Sasquatch, Kaayii. He sat on a branch hugging the slender trunk as the wind gently swayed his tree and all the lofty tops of the pine trees in the forest at the top of the mountain. Ants, centipedes and spiders that lived in its scaly brown bark scurried about their business until they got too close to the Sasquatch and he sucked them into his mouth with his flexible lips.

Only a few years older than Minnie, Kaayii was a good two feet taller, and more than twice as wide. His hair was of such a dark reddy-brown that it appeared black from a distance, covering his entire body, except for the soles of his feet, the palms of his hands, under his eyes and his wide, dark-grey nose. His forehead was covered with short dense hair growing to a prominent brow ridge above his widely spaced, deep-set eyes, which had no whites to them and were black with a dark-brown iris. His neck was thick and short; his shoulder muscles seemed to reach up to near his black, human-like ears. His head was higher at the back than the front, appearing somewhat conical with a tuft of hair at the top.

A fly circled his head and landed between his eyes. He twitched and wrinkled his nose and the fly flew away. He peered up at the pale grey cloud of smoke that filled half the sky. The eastern slopes, valleys, ridges and ravines, were punctuated by blackened tree trunks, stripped of their branches by fire, standing like slim dark monuments in the barren, shadowy landscape.

Twisting on his perch he peered out across the bay. On the far side of the water a dark glowering cloud loomed over the tree-covered hills. He watched as a jagged three-pronged fork flashed to the ground, striking the highest point on the long, green, hilly island that lay close to the opposite shore. Then there came a loud *crack!* and a deep grumbling roll of thunder.

He noticed the distant silhouette of a bird

wheeling and arching high above. Turning towards the mountain, gliding on the warm air. It was a golden eagle. As it flew overhead he could see splashes of white on the underside of its wings, the black-and-white fanned tail, and bright yellow talons.

His huge black hairy hand released its grasp on the mottled pine branch and he began to climb down from the top of the tree. He clambered down, dropping from the lower branches to the ground. A tuft of long dark hair from his arm snagged on a branch and hung there, waving gently in the breeze, the sun highlighting red hues among the dark-brown hair.

Where behind him in the tree line there had appeared to be nothing but underbrush, pine saplings and an evergreen tangle of branches, now suddenly there appeared two more, even bigger, Sasquatches, standing looking out at the fire-ravaged slopes.

His mother Yumiqsu and father Taashi stood tall and upright, with long arms hanging to their knees. They walked towards their son with slightly bent legs, a long high-stepping stride and a graceful fluid motion. Both were well over eight feet tall and covered in thick, very dark brown hair. They were thickset and broad across the chest and waist, again with no obvious neck and with heavily muscled upper back, arms and shoulders.

They stood in the tree line amongst the pines and firs beside Kaayii, and stared across the bay to where the claw of forked lightning had struck the high point of the island and where now a wisp of grey smoke curled. They lifted their huge hairy arms and pointed at the island.

Taashi then lifted his youngest child, a very young, small female Sasquatch, Yaluqwa, off her mother's back. He sniffed her head and dumped her gently on the ground. She clung to her mother's leg. Her head was round and, like her body, was covered in thick, short light-brown hair. Her skin on her face and hands and feet was a pale brown. Her big, round eyes were black with a golden-brown centre. Her teeth were small and white when she smiled at her brother Kaayii.

Klunk klunk! Two solid knocks rang out from the wooded slopes below them. A dark shape could be seen pushing through the tall brush. Soon another huge Sasquatch strode smoothly out of the pine thicket to where the group stood.

This was Kaayii's uncle, Ahniiq. He opened his black wrinkled hand and showed a pile of plump golden-currant berries. In his other hand he held a puffball mushroom, the size of a small soccer ball, creamy white with beige, scaly patches. He sensed the other Sasquatches' gratitude.

Yumiqsu, as the matriarch of the clan, gathered the berries in her hands, squatted down and spread the food on some birch bark. The Sasquatches settled down around her on the flattened grass amongst the white, pink and yellow flowers of the meadow and began to share the fruit and the mushroom.

Taashi used his son's name as he reminded him by the power of thought alone of his role in the clan that day: *Kaayii, you are day watcher.* Wiping the berry juice from his mouth with the hairy back of his hand, Kaayii stood and, in turn, gently touched the head of his father, his uncle – who grunted, his little sister who squeaked, and his mother who held his hand pressed to her forehead. As he turned to walk down the mountain, his father stepped forward, and again using mind-speak he told him: *keep your distance if you see people.*

Kaayii, like all Sasquatches, could sense the energy of the forest. As he walked he tuned in to the constant background throb of life amongst the trees, and it soothed him. His attention was alert to sensing animal energy from a long way off. If a group of deer wandered into Sasquatch territory while grazing, he knew where they were, and what they were, without even seeing, hearing or smelling them. So Kaayii knew that if a person were anywhere near, he'd be aware of them.

As he gained the soft, unbroken earth and the deep-green shade under the pines, he sensed the constant tremor of life energy in the ground beneath his feet. He knelt, put an ear to the ground and imagined the millions of hard-working insects breaking down the organic matter. He could feel the roots of all the trees and bushes taking moisture and nutrients from the ground. He could hear the underground fungus that grew a vital web of billions of thin threads linking the roots of different plants, sending nourishment where it was needed, pulsing through the veins of the earth.

Kaayii felt a sweet vague gladness in knowing

that, for this day, he was guardian of the forest and of all the creatures of the forest, whether flighted, fleet of foot, slitherers, burrowers, creepers or crawlers. They all had their place and he would help them keep it.

Pausing at a stand of juniper bushes growing near a ravine he plucked purple berries. He chewed to let the juices build up in his mouth then swallowed the tangy sweetness. As he munched the fruit he made a sound, which conveyed '*this is delicious...*' but sounded more like '*goompoop...*'

He clambered down the ravine and bounded up the other side. Feeling that he needed to run, he ran, he ran fast. The hair on his arms, legs, back and head flew out behind him, flapping and fluttering with each massive stride. Sometimes he would take a series of long arching leaps like a gazelle or a kangaroo, simply because he could, such was his immense strength and athleticism. This bounding and leaping required great concentration to ensure he always landed safely.

Stopping in a stand of mature pine trees. Kaayii put his ear to the orange-brown bark of a tree. He could hear the water carrying the sugars in the sapwood layer beneath the outer bark. It sounded like whispering and he knew by the sound of it that this was a very healthy tree. Using his strong fingers with their tough black fingernails, he prized away some bark, a piece nearly as long as his arm. He pulled at strips of the sweet white succulent inner bark. He chewed, and swallowed with relish.

Near the pine was an immense, solitary redwood tree, four times as wide as Kaayii. He eased his fingers into the deep, gnarled grooves of the soft, fibrous, red-brown bark that twisted thickly up the massive trunk, and pulled a chunk away.

He traversed two more ravines, before arriving where smooth grey granite shouldered out of the ground by a small outcrop of white quartz. The quartz was knobbly and bumpy, a dull creamy brown colour like an exposed brain, but in other places the quartz was clear and shiny, like glass. He bent down to touch it, closing his eyes and taking a moment to sense its energy.

A long, straight pine trunk had been dislodged from where it had been positioned, probably by a passing deer. Kaayii carefully replaced it, tucking it in tight to the quartz. He followed the network of precisely positioned tree trunks, each connected to the next, sometimes stacked two or three trunks high, but always touching the next one down, creating a link all the way from the quartz to the Giant X at the Aspen Grove.

Since the fire, Kaayii's clan had created these structures on this side of the mountain, and he maintained and added to them as he passed through the forest.

He touched the Giant X with both hands flat on the wood, and he could feel the energy from the quartz five hundred metres up the mountain. It was a sense of connecting, balancing with the pulses and rhythms of the forest, and with it came a sense of peace and purpose.

Squatting down he gathered wild onions, swiping up huge handfuls of the pungent greenery with their small white bulbs. He ate as he walked through the grove of slim white Aspen trees, enjoying the fluttering sound the small round leaves made when tickled by a breeze.

A crow cawed from somewhere close by, then swooped down and landed on a branch at about head height. In friendly greeting Kaayii said out loud, 'Oosh'. The crow cawed again, and flew on to the next pine down the trail.

Kaayii sensed energy stirring in the forest – it was animal energy but it was also human energy. Far off he heard laughter. He heard a clear strong knock on wood from the direction of the humans, a good solid *klunk!* A woodpecker answered the knock with a steady drumming nearby.

He moved stealthily from tree to tree, sure that he'd see them before they saw him, knowing how he could make himself disappear if he needed to by becoming one with the forest.

There on a game trail, below where he was standing in a juniper bush, was a girl and a boy human. The girl carried a stick, had a lot of curly brown hair and was taller than the boy. Kaayii, knowing how far he could throw a green pinecone, decided they were about four 'throws' away.

Kaayii moved closer, keeping his eyes on them until he could crouch behind a tangle of bushes and branches, two throws away. The girl said something that made the boy laugh so much he rolled on the ground. This made Kaayii want to creep even closer to hear their laughter and to see what was so funny. He crept through the bushes, careful where he planted his huge hairy feet.

The animal with them was a shaggy-coated dog,

like a small yellow wolf, with large floppy ears. Kaayii could see the dog moving away from the humans and being attracted towards the Watcher's Place, which was nearby, tuning in to strange new odours.

The Watcher's Place was a comfortable nest made of moss and grass amongst ferns and thick grasses. It was well hidden behind carefully positioned pine boughs and trunks of dead trees, with a good view down the mountain and across the bay. It was close to where the girl and boy had stopped, about one throw away. It smelt of Sasquatch there and he didn't want the dog to alert the boy and the girl to the Watcher's Place as they might then bring more people.

Kaayii briefly considered backing away as his father had told him to, but his curiosity got the better of him. He crept closer, sure to keep enough trees and bushes between him and them, and crawled behind a low grassy ridge. He looked at the dog through a mass of upturned tree roots and directed all his attention at the animal: *go*.

The dog stopped and looked directly at Kaayii. Gazing into the dog's brown eyes he told it again with his mind: *go*. The dog backed away with its tail between its legs, keeping its eyes on Kaayii, alarmed by the aggressive energy directed at him, like a physical push from the big hairy beast in the bushes.

The two young people were crouched down, looking at the ground, talking intently. As Kaayii watched them he began to sense from the girl something within her. He sensed she held a deep sorrow but also a strong spirit. Both energies were battling with each other and this was unbalancing her. Her spirit was so strong that when he stared intently at her he could see her energy – the air around her seemed to gleam faintly. He'd never seen or felt that from a human before. He'd seen hunters carrying killing sticks and from time to time people walking on the trails in the woods but there was something different about this one.

The girl looked in Kaayii's direction. She looked around and up in to the forest with a searching look, like she sensed they weren't alone. He watched them as they talked together, then they and the dog started back down the track towards the bay.

Kaayii stepped on to the grassy ridge to watch them as they ran, squealing and laughing, with the dog bounding on ahead. He was fascinated by the way the girl's mass of curly hair bounced and flopped as she ran, just as the dog's ears flopped and bounced.

Jumping up to grab a low branch, he climbed the nearest pine tree, scrambling up to the top in a few seconds. He could see down over the treetops on the slopes to the group of cabins near the water. A flock of seagulls was floating out in the bay and something else caught his attention – on the roof of one of the cabins, bent over with his head in his hands was a man, sitting alone.

Kaayii watched for a while. The man didn't move. Kaayii climbed down. He stepped carefully through the ferns and brush onto the trail where the young ones had been, and now he could see what it was they'd been so fascinated by – four distinct tracks in the muddy part of the trail. He recognised his own feet in the prints. Kaayii thought about how he'd been taught to try to avoid leaving any obvious signs, especially this close to people and their walking paths and their gathering place. It was very careless to leave tracks, as the last thing a Sasquatch wants is for people to know they are there.

He considered dragging a pine branch over the prints to brush them away but he was hungry again, so decided instead to find a suitable tree from which to harvest some more sweet inner bark, which was his second favourite thing to eat in the forest, after honey.

The rest of that day he watched and waited and ate soft inner bark and berries, and he dozed. He used the spongy red bark from the redwood as a headrest seated in his nest, leaning back against the pine tree. A part of him was always alert to the energy in the forest, but all day, like most days, nothing unusual happened. Birds, squirrels, mice, a sleek brown stoat, its larger cousin the pine marten and hundreds of dancing white butterflies had all passed near by. He thought about the girl, the boy and the dog, and he thought about the man on the cabin roof. They were perplexing, and they sparked a curiosity in him. He decided he would watch them from a safe distance, whenever they ventured into the forest.

When darkness fell he walked back up the

mountain and stopped to stand on an outcrop of grey rock looking back through a gap in the trees at the few lights twinkling around the bay. He could see red and white lights moving slowly across the water and wondered what they were, where they were going and why. The human world was so close, yet so strange to Kaayii.

Chapter Two

Inside the dense thicket of pine trees on High Ridge, just below the top of the mountain, was the clan meeting area. They kept it cleaned and cleared, with stacks of branches, and structures from pushed-over pine trees placed all around so that from the outside the middle was well hidden.

It was where they gathered at night to eat a kill together if they had one, or before dispersing to hunt if they hadn't. There were two family groups in the clan. His family group consisted of grandmother, Shweya, father Taashi, mother Yumiqsu, sister Yaluqwa and uncle Ahniiq. The other group in the clan was made up of three females and two males – Ahnoosh and Yaaqwun and their daughter Shumsha, and an older pair, Wesh and Enksi.

When the fire had been raging in their forest Kaayii often saw Enksi standing alone at the far edge of High Ridge looking out over the ravaged, smoking land. His eyes sparked with excitement whenever a pocket of flame took hold and the fire spread on a distant slope. Kaayii understood his interest as, like all Sasquatches, he was drawn to fire – fascinated, but afraid of its power. Kaayii remembered a long time ago, when he was very young, Enksi had dropped a pile of rocks, which somehow made a spark, which quickly lit the dry grass around. The wind spread the fire so quickly that it brought people and the Sasquatches hid and watched as the men extinguished the flames by beating them out with strange flat sticks. The clan told Enksi to be more careful. The fire that devastated their forest started a long way away but the wind blew it closer and closer, jumping rivers and ravines, forcing animals to flee ahead of it. The Sasquatches had had to leave their deep caves and find a new home. Kaayii hoped their new home might be on this mountain.

The eleven sat together, feeling safe and comfortable in each other's company. The Sasquatches used mind-speak to share simple ideas, observations and instructions, but to address a large group or a visitor from another clan, or on special occasions, or simply when excited, surprised or scared they would resort to spoken words.

Their language had been shaped over millennia: as old as the hills and as complex as the cavernous networks in the rocks beneath them – a language of musical rhythms formed in geometrical sound-shapes as complex and as perfect as crystal structure.

Kaayii spoke in this rich language, telling the clan about the boy and the girl and his footprints, and they all lobbed small sticks at him for being so careless. He tried to describe the girl and her strong spirit, and as he did so they leant in closer to hear. There was no sense of worry in the group because the boy and the girl were young and so far down the mountain.

Looking at his mother and without speaking Kaayii asked where his father was. Yumiqsu nodded at the huge pile of branches and stacked trees at the far end of the clearing. When the fire had first come and started to spread in to their territory, they had abandoned their caves and all moved up to High Ridge. They had watched the fire spread on the lower slopes until the wind changed after many, many days, but they couldn't go back – not until the grasses had grown back and the voles and the lemmings had returned to eat the grass, and the martens had returned to feed on the smaller rodents, and the larger beasts had returned and the trees and bushes had recovered. Only then could the clan return.

Although they had been looking they hadn't yet found any good caves on High Ridge or on the slopes on the bay side of the mountain. His grandmother couldn't manage the climb to their new home, and his father had carried her up to the high ground on his back. He had built her a place to rest, but not having a warm cave to sleep in at night and shelter in the day had been too much for her, and she soon became too frail to move from her sleeping den.

They'd all piled pine branches around a very old, fallen redwood trunk and pushed grass and leaves inside to keep her warm and dry. Two clan members would always sleep with her in their arms to keep her warm. It was usually her two sons Taashi and Ahniiq. To ease the passing of her spirit they would sing the ancient songs of love and of the forest and of the passing from one life to the next.

They all knew her time to pass would soon come and, that evening, when Kaayii's father emerged from the sleeping den and stood with his head hung low, the clan knew her spirit had left her body. Ahniiq hurried over and crawled into the den. Kaayii, his mother Yumiqsu and his little sister quickly gathered around Taashi and held him tight.

The moon had risen, and was glowing pearly white in the ink-black sky. Kaayii helped the others dig the earth away in the spot they had chosen, using sticks and their hands. Small rocks and stones were gathered in one pile and the rich, red-brown earth in another. When they'd dug out enough earth, they lifted her body from beside the sleeping nest and carried it in silence to its resting place.

It was close to a small quartz outcrop, amongst a stand of poplar, spruce and pine trees, with a clear view across the bay to the island. They laid her body on its side and arranged her limbs with her knees bent. They placed her favourite stick and a small piece of crystal quartz in her hands.

They all helped to pile the earth over her body and placed the stones in a circle on top. Kaayii's father and uncle carefully planted a young pine sapling on top of the pile of earth, and pressed it firmly into place.

The birds fell quiet, the wind died away, the trees stood still, nocturnal animals kept a respectful distance, and silence reigned.

Kaayii's father stood alone on the grave. Looking up to the sky, his face wet with tears, he pulled his massive hairy shoulders back, filled his lungs, and howled at the moon a mournful cry of grief and loss that resonated through the forest and beyond.

When the echoes of his voice had died away, they covered the earth with moss like an emerald green blanket and as they worked together they hummed one musical note, the same note, repeated long and low, over and over and over.

That night the Sasquatches sat around under the trees, close together. Silver patches of moonlight patterned the forest floor through the pines. There was no hunting.

Sensing animal energy nearby, Kaayii looked at his sister. *Coyotes*, he silently told her, and she held his hand tighter. Seconds later the silence was ripped apart by a high-pitched yowl, ringing out clear and strong. They all stood up as seven coyotes trotted into the clearing. Four of the coyotes had a limb of deer meat each in their jaws and they dropped them at the edge of the clearing. They were a pack of identical light-brown, long-legged coyotes with big erect ears, a narrow snout and teeth bared in an anxious grin. They held their heads and tails down meekly. Then they all lifted their heads and howled together a solemn and respectful song. When they had finished they ran off, swiftly and silently, into the forest.

If other animals left offerings of meat the Sasquatches always ate it with gratitude, and they were just settling down again on their patches of moss and grass to eat the deer meat, when the slow methodical, heavy thud, thud, thud of a bull moose was heard. His massive antlers, branching to fourteen points, and fully seven feet from tip to tip, swept low and wide from his long slim head. Threads of moss and strands of grass dangled from the points. His ears swivelled keenly and his bulging black eyes looked sorrowfully at each member of the clan, communicating sincere symapthy to them all for the recent loss of their oldest family member.

Kaayii's father stood and approached the moose. He touched his head. Over eight feet tall at the shoulder, Kaayii's father looked him in the eye. Extending his huge black hand he gave the moose two big plant bulbs with waxy green leaves attached. Soon white spittle oozed from the moose's mouth as he chomped down on them, and Kaayii's father gently led him away so he wouldn't dribble on their clean sitting place.

Chapter Three

Low light sparked in silver shards off dew-covered grass and ferns lining the trail. Newly woven spiders' webs shimmered between the branches of the juniper bushes as Kaayii and his father walked down the mountain to the Watcher's Place before dawn, bringing the remains of one of the deer legs with them.

Daytime forest creatures stirred. Mice scurried through the yellow meadow flowers, crows and blue jays chattered tetchily at each other in the vivid green branches of the hemlock trees.

Kaayii knelt to suck water droplets off the grass, and to let his father walk about two 'throws' ahead of him. He sensed that his father was still grieving and needed time alone.

When they reached the Watcher's Place his father dumped the deer leg on the grass and asked silently: *where?* Kaayii pointed directly down the slope. Placing his feet with care, his father walked down the trail and looked at the footprints still clearly imprinted in the dark soil.

He climbed a nearby pine tree pulling himself up with his massive arms, shoulder, and back muscles hoisting himself into the 'V' of a strong branch. Kaayii sat on the grass and started eating the deer meat. His father's weight made the pine tree creak and groan, swaying back and forth as he moved high above, looking down on the trees, the cabins by the bay, and across the water to the mist-shrouded island and hills beyond.

There was a large pile of open brown pinecones near the Watcher's Place. A squirrel must have collected them and picked out the pine nuts.

Knowing that people might see the pile and be curious about it, Kaayii took up a short branch and started clearing black and grey pinecones. A squirrel in a tree nearby chattered angrily at Kaayii.

His father dropped to the ground from the tree, landing softly and rubbing the sticky pine resin from his hands onto his hairy arms and chest. Sasquatches love the scent of pine resin. He joined Kaayii and, grabbing the deer leg, he started to eat. Taashi passed bits of meat to his son, tearing them off the bone with his teeth. He wiped his mouth with the back of his huge hand, and looking at his son he spoke, and his words meant, 'With people in this forest, our clan must journey on.' His father's speaking voice was so gruff, so deep, close and full that it resonated in Kaayii's chest, and it thrilled him. Taashi looked at his son, and Kaayii grunted in agreement, 'Hmm...'

They sat together, tuned in to the forest, alert to every sound and sensation carried by the wind, the earth, the living plants and animals; eating wild onions and meat as the sun rose. The flat light in the shadow of the mountain lifted. His father put a hand on Kaayii's knee and communicated one thought: *people,* and Kaayii too sensed the approach of human energy.

They rose to stand behind separate pine trees in front of a dense, dark tangle of bushes, tall grasses and underbrush. Kaayii's pine tree was only half as wide as his chest and his father was three times as wide as the tree he was standing behind, but they knew that against the backdrop of tangled underbrush they were virtually invisible to people.

It was the same girl and a man. Kaayii saw the killing stick in the man's hand. Focusing his attention on the man, he sensed there was not a strong connection between the man and the forest.

Kaayii's father silently told him: *stay*, as he moved to a group of tall bushes. Kaayii could hear the people talking. The girl had sat down right by the footprints and they were looking at them as they talked. The girl was talking louder and seemed to be getting angry with the man.

Kaayii watched his father reach up and twist a green pinecone off a branch. Leaning out from behind the tree, he took aim, and lobbed the pinecone. It arched through the air hitting the man on the shoulder. They argued more and Kaayii sensed the man was now fearful as he quickly turned and, followed by the girl, he walked away down the slope.

Good throw, Kaayii told his father when he joined him in the hidden mossy nest.

His father dozed beside him in the Watcher's Place when, ink black and silent, the crow swooped out of nowhere, down through branches, and settled softly right in front of Kaayii's face on a bouncing bough. Vivid yellow crow eyes looked at black

Sasquatch smiling eyes that blinked in greeting. 'Oosh,' said Kaayii.

The crow communicated one thought to Kaayii: *wolf*.

Without waking his father, he stood and followed the crow as it flew off through the trees. He began to sense 'wolf' and scanned the slopes all around. The crow cawed from somewhere at the edge of his hearing. He ran. It was a leaping, bounding run, pushing aside branches and shouldering away saplings. He cut across trails and leapt off rocky outcrops. He was a blur of energy darting through the trees.

Suddenly, there ahead on the trail, stood one black wolf. The wolf's coat was thick and shiny with brown patches on the chest. He had twice the bulk of a coyote, with a broader snout and smaller ears. He looked so sturdy, strong and proud that Kaayii stopped one throw away to assess him. The wolf calmly stared at the Sasquatch. *We are many,* communicated the wolf.

As are we, Kaayii told him. *Why here?* he asked the wolf.

An image of high flames licking at tall trees entered Kaayii's mind from the wolf.

Kaayii bent down and lifted a short length of tree branch as thick as his wrist. With it he pointed north and as he did, he told the wolf: *go, go away*.

The wolf did not go, it did not turn and run away, as Kaayii had directed, but fixed him with his bright yellow eyes, then in a trice he turned and padded away, not due north, but down the slope towards the bay. Kaayii threw the heavy stick at the retreating wolf. It thumped in to a pine tree near the wolf's head and the wolf stopped and turned slowly to look at him, its thick, long black tail flicking angrily. Then it lolloped off down the trail, and round a bend, disappearing into the underbrush.

That night when Kaayii and his father returned to the meeting place his father made him describe what happened with the wolf to the whole clan as they sat around eating berries, onion plants, mushrooms and deer meat. His uncle Ahniiq stood up and told the clan: *I will fight them!*

Yumiqsu stood, put her hand on Ahniiq's shoulder and made him sit down. Ahniiq stared at

Kaayii and threw a mushroom at him to get his attention: *show me this wolf.*

When the clan dispersed, either to hunt or to rest, Kaayii took his father's hand and led him to the edge of the clearing. It was a warm night. They stood in dappled moonlight under the trees. Kaayii chose his words carefully and their meaning was, 'We can not leave this place to the wolves. People are close by.'

Taashi turned to look at his son. The moon sparked briefly in his black eyes as he blinked.

'Ahniiq will remain here to balance the forest.'

Kaayii loosed his grip on his father's hand and placed the palms of his hands flat on his father's massive chest and looked up into his face.

'Ahniiq does not love this forest. He holds too much anger from the fire to love this new place.'

Taashi held his son's earnet gaze. 'You choose your words well, Kaayii.'

Gazing up at the half-full moon, as white as a puffball mushroom, his father's voice rumbled in the depths of his chest.

'When we see the moon is full, we go. Ahniiq, he stays.'

Chapter Four

Before dawn Kaayii left the clan among the dense pines on High Ridge and walked down to the Watcher's Place. He could tread very softly when he wanted to and when he did so the animals of the forest would go about their business foraging, feeding and fighting – doing whatever their instincts led them to.

A raccoon rambled by, crossing his path, his eyes set in a mask of black fur, his grey-and-white ringed tail twitching as he marked out his territory with his raccoony scent.

An owl swooped, ghostly grey and silent, flying low over Kaayii and disappearing into the forest, its night hunting done.

He heard a grunting in a bush followed by a 'teeth clicking' sound. Kaayii found a short branch and threw it at the bush. An angry black porcupine backed out, proffering its dozens of white-tipped quills. Kaayii moved on.

A flash of colour caught his eye as a pine jay

with vivid bright-blue wings and tail, and a crest of black feathers on the top of its head, flitted from branch to branch in a mulberry bush, pecking at the fruit. Kaayii reached up and plucked the dark ripe berries, thanking the bird for showing him.

He took a longer route than usual to the Watcher's Place, one that avoided the first two ravines. As he walked, he began to sense the busy energy of bees nearby. He waited, then he saw them, coming and going, collecting nectar from the fluffy white blossom of the green clover carpeting the forest floor.

He followed the hum of the dancing bees from the alders they were foraging under, all the way back to their nest in a hollow halfway up an oak tree, not far from the Aspen Grove.

Kaayii climbed up and carefully reached in to break off some of the waxy, sticky honeycomb. The bees crawled all over his arms but his covering of long hairs meant they couldn't sting him. Climbing down with his hunk of honeycomb dripping from his hand, he supped on it greedily, licking at the sweetness as it oozed through his fingers.

He was still sucking his fingers clean when he settled down in the Watcher's Place. Nothing much happened that morning, but as he was about to doze off his uncle Ahniiq approached, communicating one questioning thought: *wolf?*

Kaayii led him the same way the crow had led him the day before, jogging through the pines, oaks and beech trees, leaping over bushes and fallen branches.

Kaayii retrieved the stick he'd thrown at the wolf from where it lay beneath an alder tree, and they set off together through the dew-heavy grass, and cobwebby underbrush, following the dark wolf's tracks.

The crow swooped down, settling on a branch. Kaayii asked with his mind: *wolves?* The crow flew off cawing, as if asking the other creatures the same question.

They followed the trail of scent markings the wolf had left on trees and outcrops of rocks, claiming the territory as his, and each scent marking they met angered his uncle more.

Between the trees flashed a view of the bay as they jogged along a winding trail, following the tracks and the scent. The track abruptly cut away up an incline. Before long they had looped back round to the Aspen Grove. They stopped on the edge of it. No sign of wolf and the forest was quiet. The tracks skirted the outside of the grove.

There was a strong odour of wolf at the Giant X. It had lingered there, leaving its scent on both of the pine trunks. This enraged his uncle, who raced ahead of Kaayii, headlong in to the thicket where the wolf's tracks clearly led.

Kaayii stopped abruptly, sensing animal energy, but it was not wolf, it was dog. A second later the yellow dog was running towards him through the aspens.

Kaayii sprinted in to the thicket after his uncle, catching up to him he grabbed his arm: *people*!

Ahniiq stopped and turned, searching for movement, for people. They crouched low in the brush and listened. Peering down the slope through the branches of trees they could now see the dog sniffing around under the Giant X. Then the girl and man appeared, walking through the brush towards the aspens. Ahniiq glanced at Kaayii: *people*!

Ahniiq hid behind a redwood tree, the wolf now forgotten, and peered round it fascinated by what he was seeing. The man and the girl looked closely at the Giant X, the marker for the start of

Sasquatch territory. Trotting to where the wolf had laid its scent, the dog sniffed the pine trunk and backed away, alarmed by what it smelt. Then it followed the Sasquatch scent through the brush up the slope.

Ahniiq stepped out from behind the tree and hurried towards the dog. Kaayii broke cover and on all fours, keeping low to the ground, raced his uncle to the dog. Hidden from the sight of the people they crashed through the brush. Ahniiq was about to scoop up the yellow dog when Kaayii leapt forward and grabbed the dog out of his hands. It barked in surprise but Kaayii held him firmly. *Kill it,* was Ahniiq's one command.

The dog yelped and wriggled in Kaayii's strong arms. Ahniiq watched the humans intently from behind a stand of pines as Kaayii grappled with the dog. He put the dog on the ground, holding him down, and looking in his eyes communicated: *friend.* Then he let him go and the panicked yellow dog disappeared into the brush with its tail between its legs.

Searching among the leaves and dead branches that littered the forest floor, Ahniiq picked up two rocks in his massive hairy black hands. He smashed them together. *CLACK!* They watched the humans' reactions. As they didn't immediately turn and start walking back the way they came, Ahniiq clacked them together twice more. *CLACK CLACK!* The humans were still just talking! Kaayii couldn't understand why they weren't retreating. Ahniiq was now muttering and rocking from side to side – a sign of his increasing agitation.

Ahniiq leant against the nearest tall, slim tree, pushing with his hands on the trunk with his arms out in front of him and rocked the tree back and forth until roots started to snap with a dull, muffled *clunk* under ground – *clunk, clunk, clunk.* Finally there was a *cracking* and a *crashing* as the tree gave up its grip on the earth and violently smashed through branches, flattening saplings, and *thumping* on to the floor of the forest with a loud *WHUMP!*

The man and the girl were leaving now, and quickly. The forest fell deathly silent and the two enormous Sasquatches disappeared into the undergrowth without a sound.

Chapter Five

As Kaayii was on day-watcher duties he was allowed to sleep at night in his grandmother's sleeping den while the other clan members were foraging, hunting or eating. It was well insulated against any breeze – the wind, baffled by the thick pile of pine boughs stacked carefully against the vast fallen redwood tree, and the dried grass and moss shoved in between the branches, made it like a giant bird's nest, all snug and soft and warm.

Early pre-dawn birdsong woke Kaayii from his slumber. Near his head were three small white eggs, and a large pile of red and purple berries, which he began to pop into his mouth as he lay on his back, looking at the thin shafts of grey light penetrating the tangle of branches.

He crawled out into the soft low light of dawn with the eggs in his hand. His mother and little sister Yaluqwa were looking at him from their sitting place against a redwood tree. His sister's big brown eyes sparkled with mischief as she smiled at him. He popped an egg into his mouth and crunched. He thought how Yaluqwa's face had more downy soft brown hair over her cheeks and chin than last time he'd really looked at her. *You're growing fast*, he thought. He held an egg in his hand for her and she rushed over and grabbed it deftly out of his big, black, wrinkled palm.

She immediately ran to the nest under the redwood muttering her babyish noises, and disappeared in to the cave-like darkness. Kaayii smiled, knowing she would learn to speak soon and was practising making sounds and shapes with her mouth. At this age she was communicating by thought alone, and her mother was exhausted by the constant garbled questions. *Take your sister with you.* She implored him. *It is not safe*, he quickly responded, holding his mother's hand. *People*, he reminded her.

His mother smiled and crawled in to the sleeping nest, and as she disappeared into the darkness she asked him to bring some onion plants back with him. His little sister clambered over her mother, looked at Kaayii with a serious expression and said, 'Ploop!'

At the onion patch beneath the Giant X, Kaayii pulled up clumps of the plant. When he had his arms full of the floppy green leaves he ran back. Running smoothly, steadily, with browny-red hair streaming out behind him, he charged all the way back up the mountain to deliver the onions to his mother.

Dumping the pile of now drooping onion plants outside the nest he immediately ran back down the mountain taking the most direct route – down and up the three ravines. When he got back to the Aspen Grove, not far from the Watcher's Place, he remembered the tree his uncle had pushed over in a rage. He went to find it.

It was a birch tree: its peeling bark, smooth and white, black and knotty; its jagged roots with earth stuck on them. He set to cleaning up the tree by ripping off the branches and piling them up together. He started pulling off all the bark. He chewed on strips of the fleshy white inner layer as he worked and stacked the rest of the bark in a neat pile.

Knocking off the earth from around the roots, he hoisted the tree on to his shoulder. In a clearing ringed by giant redwood trees was a huge structure of six tree trunks leaning together like the supports of a teepee. He lowered one end of the birch to the ground, and raised the other end. He was careful to fit the birch trunk in securely so it added to the strength of the structure, wouldn't fall in a storm and would withstand being pushed by a bear looking for something to scratch its back against.

Kaayii moved to the top of the clearing where there was another X, to look at the 'blind'. It had been built by carefully weaving and threading branches large and small, knitting them together into a strong tall barrier. It was impossible for a deer to jump over or get through, forcing them to go round it.

Whilst most of the time they just ate roots, shoots, nuts, mushrooms and fruit, when it was time for a deer to pass to the next life the Sasquatches would use a 'blind' to hide behind. As Kaayii worked he remembered the last hunt with his father, his uncle and two members of the clan. Two of the Sasquatches advanced on a deer, a few 'throws' apart, edging it closer to the ambush. Then using the lowest deepest sound they could make in the depths of their chest, they put the deer into a trembling trance with a magical vibration in the air that some animals couldn't even hear. Then his father approached the deer and its passing was instant and painless, its life honoured with solemn words of gratitude.

Kaayii sat behind the blind. Happy with his work, he decided to take a nap and he stretched out on his back with his hands behind his head.

He was suddenly awakened by the crow. *Caw … caw!* It was perched on the blind, looking at Kaayii with its beady yellow eyes, still bright as jewels in the low light of late afternoon. *People,* it told him. He was on his feet in a flash, and crouching behind the blind he peeped over the top. Yes, he could sense human energy *and* dog energy.

The yellow dog bursting out of the underbrush on the far side of the clearing raced towards the high, pointed structure in the centre and started sniffing eagerly. Now he could hear the girl calling for the dog. He tried saying the name she kept calling, '*Musto*'. He pondered what it might mean, 'small yellow wolf'?

Through the tangled web of sticks and tree limbs, Kaayii spied the girl as she emerged into the clearing. She shrieked when she saw the seven-trunked teepee structure, and to Kaayii she looked happy and surprised. She touched the very same birch trunk that Kaayii had carefully secured in place. She pushed it, and of course it was rock solid.

The dog stood right in front of the blind sniffing the air, looking right at Kaayii, directly into his black eyes. Kaayii hummed the deepest sound he could, looking at the dog to see what would happen. The dog started to tremble, his yellow fur quivering. Kaayii was pleased that his deep hum worked so well. He wondered whether this creature smelled like a wolf.

He told the dog: *here, now!* The yellow dog crawled into a narrow gap in the blind and wriggled itself through, and Kaayii grabbed it by the scruff of the neck and slid to the ground amongst the tall grass. He sniffed its neck – no, nothing like a wolf. Kaayii thought the dog smelled of forest mud. He licked the dog's coat and there was a faint trace of salty sea deep in the fur.

Kaayii stood up in the bushes with the dog held

tightly between his legs. He could see the girl gazing into the blind. She must have been affected by his 'deep hum' because she just stood there not moving. He picked up a stick and, hurling it at a redwood on the side of the clearing, it made a solid *clunk* against the bark of the tree.

Kaayii and the dog dashed away up the slope through the underbrush. The dog wagged his tail foolishly, jumping up and licking Kaayii's hand. They ran together and the dog barked and barked.

Kaayii took off down the ravine and up the other side as fast as he could. Just before he leapt behind a large juniper bush, he glanced back to see Musto cresting the top of the ravine. He slowed to let the dog catch up.

Then he heard a short sharp scream.

Chapter Six

The girl lay at the bottom of the ravine. Peering down from the edge, Kaayii could see blood on a rock near her head.

Closely followed by the dog, he ran quickly down. The dog was fussing over the girl, fretting and agitated. It tried to wake her by licking her face. Kaayii lifted her up in his long hairy arms and carried her to the top of the ravine. He gathered up some leaves and grasses and laid her gently down.

With a handful of moss he wiped the blood from her head. Seeing that her hand was bleeding from a cut, he wiped that clean too. He found a large smooth flat leaf and placed it under her cheek to keep the soil off her face. He looked at her closely. He put his huge hair-covered face close to hers and smelt her breath. With one long, black and wrinkly finger he touched her smooth and hairless face. No wrinkles! This was very strange to Kaayii, and he imagined she must always have a cold face, because it was bald. Her skin was a smooth golden brown with freckles on it, a scattering of light-brown dots across her nose and cheeks. He touched her curly brown hair, which felt softer than moss, softer even than bird feathers. He sniffed her hair. It smelt fruity so he licked it. It tasted of nothing. He knew humans were very strange-looking but to see one up close was fascinating.

He couldn't stop staring at this bizarre-looking creature and the more he looked the more his heart ached because he knew she was sad about something. He thought it must be because she had to go back to living in one of those big human nests with straight, hard-looking sides that light up from the inside at night. When she wasn't in one of those she would be stuck in the ones that moved somehow, on things that looked like round rocks. He worried for her. He worried that her life was always going to mean she had to leave the forest, leave the energy of plants and animals and grieve for that loss again and again.

He broke a thick branch to a good swinging length and, wanting other Sasquatches to come to where he was quickly, Kaayii knocked loudly three times on a tall straight pine tree – KLONK! KLONK! KLONK!

A short while later there were two distant answering knocks from the near the top of the mountain – klonk! klonk!

As Kaayii waited three squirrels gathered in a nearby pine and shouted at him, the girl and the dog for being in their territory, 'cheek! cheek!' they yelled. He practised his throwing by lobbing sticks and old pinecones at the squirrels and this made them even noisier.

To direct the approaching Sasquatches to where he was, from time to time he whacked a tree just once, loudly, with his stout stick – KLONK!

The girl began to stir. She moaned. Kaayii quickly hurried behind a large bush and the dog followed him. On all fours, he began to crawl away through the underbrush. Sticking close to his side, the dog kept jumping up at him and sniffing him all over and he understood why the dog would love the smell of a Sasquatch, because the girl smelt of nothing very interesting.

The next ravine was really steep, with loose flat rocks scattered about its edges. After a couple of tentative attempts, the dog stayed where it was, pacing back and forth at the top and barking at Kaayii, who'd climbed down to the stony gully at the bottom.

Night was closing in on the forest, in the gloom under the canopy of high pine trees. The moon was still low in the sky, hidden by cloud cover, and the wind barely troubled the tops of the pines. Down on the forest floor, all was still. Kaayii sensed Sasquatches approaching and his father and mother appeared at the top of the ravine and looked down at him.

A human is hurt, he communicated to them and they hurried down into the ravine and up the other side with Kaayii.

The two older Sasquatches towered over the shaggy yellow dog cowering behind Kaayii. To the dog in the fading twilight they were vast hulking shadows that smelt very strange.

His father picked up the dog by the scruff of the neck and looked at him closely: *small smelly yellow wolf?*

Kaayii led the way back through the darkening forest towards where he'd left the girl. They trod carefully and quietly, the noisiest by far being the dog, which trotted along with a foolish grin, kicking up leaves like it was on a regular walk in the woods.

Kaayii spoke the name of the dog out loud for his parents in his deep rich voice, 'Musto'. Then used language to explain. 'His name is Musto. It is yellow in the human language. He is yellow like the tall grass in winter. Yellow. Musto.'

'Musto!' they repeated, and both parents laughed so much they farted, and this made them laugh even more, shouldering each other playfully off the path and giggling.

Kaayii watched his parents, wondering at their behaviour, then realised this was the first time they'd left the clan together in many days. Not since the fire had driven them away from their caves. His father had not left the side of Kaayii's dying grandmother for more than a few moments in her last days and Kaayii's mother always had Yaluqwa clinging to her, so this must be a welcome change for them.

They stopped behind a pair of pine trees near

the top of the first ravine, watching the girl as she pulled things from her bag, stumbling slightly on the uneven rocky ground. It was almost completely dark now and easy for them to hide from the girl amongst the trees.

They watched as she crawled under the low branches of a large pine tree. Kaayii held the dog, and they crouched down and waited.

His father nudged Kaayii in the ribs, nodding in the girl's direction. Kaayii understood and so let the dog go. Musto ran straight to the girl's tree crashing through the underbrush, sniffing and circling it, looking for a way in. It pushed in through the branches.

Yumiqsu grasped Taashi's arm, and soon Taashi silently disappeared off into the trees.

Yumiqsu and Kaayii crept closer to the girl's tree. They could hear her talking to the dog. They sat cross-legged on the ground in the now total darkness, focusing their attention on the human girl behind the curtain of pine boughs, sending her calming energy. They waited. Soon they could sense that she was in a deep sleep.

Taashi returned with the two plants Yumiqsu had told him with her mind to find. In one hand he had some dark strips of bark, and in the other a handful of juniper needles. Yumiqsu put the soft green needles in her mouth and started to chew. She peeled the bark away from the inner layer and rubbed off the dark resin from the papery dark outer bark. She held the resin in her hand, rubbing her palms together until it heated up, becoming soft and sticky. Then, fishing out the juniper needles from her mouth, she mixed the mushy green needles in with the resin in the palm of her huge black hand.

Kaayii and his mother lifted a pine bough and crawled into the space near the sleeping girl. Their long hairy legs stuck out from under the branches. Taashi must have thought it would be amusing to tickle their huge feet, because Kaayii had to kick his father's fluttering hands away, and so did his mother, muttering angrily.

Kaayii stroked Musto to keep him quiet. He was curled up next to the girl with his head on her shoulder, watching warily. Yumiqsu wiped blood from the cut on the girl's head with some damp moss, then applied the sticky, green-black goo to the cut on her head, pressing it onto the cut with her finger. She did the same with the cut on the girl's hand. When she'd finished they crawled out from under the branches, leaving a pile of the inner white strips of bark beside the girl.

The three Sasquatches sat back under low branches, against three pine trees nearby. *There is honey*, thought Kaayii, and he pointed into the darkening forest.

Kaayii stood up, and as he did so he sensed animal energy approaching. He peered in to the darkness up the trail. He could see clearly that six deer were grazing on the slope above him, making their way down towards the Sasquatches. There were four does, one spotted fawn and one stag.

Down-wind of the deer, the Sasquatches' scent wasn't detected by the deer's black, ever-twitching nostrils. They kept on nibbling delicately at low growing shoots, unaware of the presence of the three massive creatures just yards away from them. The stag, his antlers draped with bits of twig and leaf caught on the pointed ends, led the way.

Munching on a patch of young sprouting fern

shoots, bright green and still tightly curled, one doe lifted her head with huge, comically large ears to listen while the others, heads down, kept grazing. Then another would look up, her eyes rimmed with black, proud but wary. She'd listen for a few seconds before lowering her head to feed.

The deer worked through the stand of ferns but suddenly they all stopped and looked back up the mountain. Their black nostrils twitched, their big ears flicked. After a few silent seconds they resumed grazing. The Sasquatches stayed as still as statues as the deer, on their long slim legs, elegantly stepped over the ferns, picking their way carefully through the forest.

When the deer were all grouped right by the tree where the girl slept, and only a few feet away from the Sasquatches, Kaayii's father, sitting unseen under his pine tree simply opened his mouth and uttered, 'Oosh,' and in a second, and a flash of white tails, the startled deer were gone. The Sasquatches chuckled together.

A twig snapped somewhere in the dark. The Sasquatches looked up the slope, peering into the darkness. Squirrels had started chattering and calling to each other an alarm call that the birds took up, like the crow – *caw caw!* And the owl – *hoooot!*

The Sasquatches caught a glimpse of a murky shape in the shadows slipping from underbrush to tree, moving stealthily down the same slope as the deer. It was a mountain lion. He was sniffing the air, finding the scent of deer threading through the night. The cat stopped suddenly, bracing his two front legs, his paws digging in to the soft duff. He sniffed, and sniffed again as an unexpected scent invaded his senses. It was very alarming to the big cat as Sasquatches smell like nothing else in the forest.

Kaayii looked at the lion's huge clawed feet and yellow fangs in his mouth and thought of the serious damage they could do, even to a massively powerful Sasquatch. Kaayii's father rose from his haunches, unfolding his huge body, slowly standing up to his full height of eight feet two and a half inches from the padded soles of his feet to the top of his conical skull. 'Humph!' he grunted.

The cat's head flicked round to look at the massive hairy beings, keeping his body low, head down, his tail swiping left and right.

Knowing it was scenting the girl and the dog, Kaayii picked up a rock, as Taashi and Yumiqsu grabbed heavy branches and stepped out from under their pine tree. The cat was between them and the sleeping girl's tree. The cat sniffed the earth below the branches, ignoring the three Sasquatches.

Kaayii knew that hunger makes animals very bold and that this cat could easily choose to swoop in under the branches to grab the girl in his jaws and run away in to the dark-shrouded forest. He lifted his hand, drew his arm back and was on the point of hurling his rock, when from a great distance the song of a wolf rang out, piercing the still night air – the howl was long and anguishing. The lion reacted by swinging his head round, swivelling his ears in the direction of the wolf call.

Kaayii took his chance and loosed the rock. The rock hit its flank, it yelped and sprang back flailing with his huge clawed paws, baring his teeth as he growled and hissed. His father leapt at the cat jabbing it hard in the neck with the branch. Kaayii's mother whacked the thick end of a branch against the nearest tree loudly – KLONK! KLONK! KLONK!

The cat backed angrily away as the three Sasquatches advanced towards it. It scampered off growling and snarling and slipped away into the shadows.

Suddenly the clouds parted and the moon bathed the forest floor in gleaming silvery tones, lighting the haunches of the cat as it hurried away through the underbrush, his pride bruised and his stomach still empty.

The three Sasquatches crouched down by the tree and listened to the girl's breathing. Kaayii very gently poked his stick under a low branch and pulled it aside. The moonlight through the trees made jagged, striped shadows across the forest floor and across the sleeping girl's face. The dog, his head still on her shoulder, was awake and his eyes flitted from one huge beast to another. Kaayii let the branch swing back and they backed away from the tree.

They heard a crashing sound somewhere up the mountain, like a herd of moose galumphing through the forest, thundering through brush and stomping down the game trails. Kaayii's father muttered, 'Ahniiq,' and sure enough, Kaayii's uncle came bounding down the trail with the young female from the clan, Shumsha. Both were carrying sturdy sticks.

Ahniiq gazed at his brother, noisily snapping branches away at head height: *wolf?*

Kaayii's father held up both his hands, telling him: *quiet!*

Where is the wolf? Ahniiq demanded.

No wolf, they told him. Yumiqsu and Shumsha stayed by the tree, as Taashi and Kaayii led Ahniiq away down the trail.

Ahniiq was unsettled and kept stopping and looking back up the trail. The forest fell silent as they walked, the birds settled down, the squirrels stopped chattering.

Come, Taashi told his brother.

They walked quickly, his father and uncle ahead, with Kaayii keeping a few paces behind. They came to the first big X, and then on through the Aspen Grove and on to the the Giant X.

Taashi looked at his brother as they walked. *People are on the ancient trail.* He took Ahniiq's hand and they jogged down the slope towards the bay, making very little noise, keeping to the dark earth of the game trails and the thick grass of the underbrush, Kaayii following in their footsteps.

They stopped at the top of the main trail and all three chose a pine tree to climb. From high up they could look down on the cluster of cabins by the bay. They could see Connie's car by her cabin, the wind turbine with its four slim blades glowing brightly in the moonlight, the vegetable garden with the tall deer fence all round it, and the jetty jutting out in to the bay, with two small boats moored to it. The tide was in and waves splashed against the rocks. A strong breeze blew across the bay and they smelt salt water and seaweed.

Ahniiq communicated one thought: *fish*. He began to climb down his tree. *No!* Kaayii's father insisted and hurriedly clambered down his pine tree. He dropped to the ground as his brother was already moving down the trail. Taashi grabbed Ahniiq's arm: *no!*

Ahniiq grumbled and growled, muttering about wanting yummy fish, seaweed, and oysters, as Kaayii dropped from his tree and helped his father push Ahniiq up the trail ahead of them, away from the sea, and away from the people.

MINNIE

Chapter Twelve

The forest came alive, stimulated by the light of a new day. Minnie, curled up in her pine-needle nest, woke from a deep and restful sleep, feeling as fresh and happy as she could remember being since her mother had passed. Her first thought was not 'Where am I?' but, 'I slept all night in the forest.'

The birds sang, whistled and chirped, and squirrels chattered and trilled to each other as they scampered along branches and leapt from tree to tree. Minnie just sat, encircled by the curtain of low-hanging fir branches, and listened to the forest outside her little den, feeling completely at peace.

She vaguely remembered dreaming about her mother – that she was with her mother in the woods, not next to her but somehow just *around*, floating like a morning mist through the trees, keeping watch over her.

Her sleep-drowsy mind began to clear and she realised she was alone. Musto was not with her. 'Oh no, not again!' she said.

She noticed a hard smear of black on her hand, and only then she remembered falling, cutting her head and her hand. There was dried blood on her hands and her head was throbbing slightly. She felt an egg-shaped lump on her skull amongst her tightly curled hair and something hard stuck to it.

Something was embedded in the pine needles under the branches, and she pulled up thin, white strips of wood. She sniffed at them and nibbled at one end – it tasted sweet. She was hungry, so she chewed on it. She crawled out from under the nest of branches, pulling her backpack with her and squinting in the low, flat glow of early morning light. 'Did I dream that Musto was here?' she wondered.

Minnie now saw that the massive fir tree she had slept under, and it was by far the biggest one around, had five tall straight tree trunks, stripped of their bark, leaning into it. She looked around. 'Structures,' she said. She was surrounded by carefully positioned, stripped-bare tree trunks and branches. There were boxed off areas on the ground where the forest floor was clean – cleared of undergrowth, leaf litter and fallen twigs, and the earth pressed down flat.

Under the nearest three pine trees moss had been gathered in huge piles, and appeared to have been sat on, or lain on, by something large. There were three of these mossy 'nests' and as she looked around she could see that in places the duff under the pines on the game trails was disturbed and roughed up.

'Musto!' she yelled. Silence. An eerie sense of not being alone began to creep over her. She had a distinct feeling that she was being watched. She hoped it was Musto, looking at her from somewhere nearby in the bushes, but she heard nothing, and saw nothing move.

'Caw!' called the crow from a branch directly above her.

'Oh, it's you! Great,' said Minnie. '*You've* been watching me. Go on then, tell 'em I'm here.' And the crow spread its wings and lifted from the branch. It disappeared through the trees, and she could hear its call growing fainter as it flew higher up the mountain.

Then, *klunk!* A clear wood knock rang out in the still morning air.

'Well, that wasn't Musto,' she thought. She looked directly up at the white sky between the pine treetops. 'Mom, what should I do?' she said out loud. 'If I walk downhill I will come to the bay in the end, but I can't leave without Musto.'

There were a lot of tracks on the ground, so many she couldn't differentiate between them. As she knelt to examine them a sound she knew well came from far down in the forest, but it was so faint she feared she was imagining it. It was Musto's bark! It was his excited bark. She heard it again and it was getting closer. 'Musto!' she called out as loud as she could.

'What if he's being chased by a wolf or a bear?' It was unlikely, as there was very little wildlife in this forest, apart from squirrels and birds, as far as she knew. She climbed the nearest tree anyway, just to be safer. Then she heard a voice. It was a man's voice. It was Dan, yelling her name!

'Here! Here Dan! I'm here!' Musto came bounding up the trail, his tail wagging madly, his bark ringing out through the forest.

'Minnie!' called Dan, still out of sight. She climbed down from the tree and Musto jumped up at her. She held him and hugged him, crying tears of joy and relief. Dan jogged up the trail panting heavily, rifle in hand, grabbed her and hugged her so hard she thought she might break.

'Dan! I'm sorry. I'm so sorry!'

'It's OK, Minnie. It's OK.'

'I went to Connie's … this morning…' between breaths he spluttered out. 'You weren't there … she said you didn't stay over … but your bed wasn't slept in … then Musto comes screaming out of the woods barking like crazy and he makes me follow him…'

While he caught his breath, Minnie tried to explain. 'I'm sorry, Dan. I wanted to make a special meal but I needed some onions…'

'Onions?' asked Dan.

'Yes. It's in the recipe, so I came up here with Musto. Well, down there a-ways. It grows in the Aspen Grove, under the Giant X. But he ran off after something and I followed and…'

'What did he run after?' Dan asked, looking at Musto.

'I don't know. Then I slipped and fell…'

'What's that on your head?' Dan touched her head.

'That's where I cut my head.'

'What's that stuff?' he asked.

'I don't know. I woke up with it on my head and my hand, where I cut myself.'

Dan now started looking around, looking at the disturbed ground, and up the trails, and up in to the trees.

Dan pulled her pencil from a pocket. 'I found this. You woke up with that black stuff on your cuts? What is it?'

'I dunno,' she said. Dan held her hand and sniffed at the black stuff.

'Pine resin maybe?' He touched the hard resin on her head. 'And you didn't put this on?'

'No, but Dan, I was fine! I slept under there, with Musto! He found me and we kept each other warm.' Dan looked around at all the structures leaning this way and that, at the cleaned and clear area, boxed in by straight trunks with no leaf litter or random twigs, all neat and tidy. He examined the large indentations made in the moss piles, picking them apart and sniffing them.

'Eeuw … No animals came around?' he said, and he stuck his head under the low fir boughs of the tree where she'd slept.

'No. Nothing happened,' she said, still hugging Musto. 'It was all quiet. Peaceful. Well, I think I woke up once, or I might have dreamed it: three loud knocks.'

Dan knelt down on one knee, scrutinising the tracks around the tree. 'Well, this is deer. A whole bunch by the look of it. But they can be pretty quiet.'

'Oh?' said Minnie, as she fussed over Musto.

'But this…' He crouched low to the ground and followed tracks on the earth. 'This is a cat, and a big one.' Minnie bent down to peer at the print.

'Oh … that's big, it's like…'

'Like, bigger than my fist.' He followed the cat tracks. 'But it goes off this way and the deer went off that way.' He looked at Minnie. 'You heard nothing last night?'

'Yup.'

'Nothing?' he asked again.

'No, nothing. Just the usual night-time kinda rustling … but that's the wind and…' Dan was still searching the ground all around. He stopped.

'Minnie? Um, this … take a look at this.'

She looked. 'OK. So…' she began, 'a really large homeless person must have, like, chased off the mountain lion?'

151

'After applying some kind of plant-based antiseptic salve to your wounds,' said Dan wryly as he lifted his rifle and scanned the trees, 'whilst you slept under that tree.'

Minnie whispered, 'I'm really hungry…'

Dan whispered, 'Shall we…?'

'Yup…' was her immediate reply. As they backed out of the area a pinecone flew past Dan's head.

'Quick! Let's go!' They didn't run, but walked *very briskly* back down the trail.

'Thank you!' she called out. 'Thank you for helping me! We're leaving now.' A pinecone whistled past her head. 'OK! We're going!'

They hurried all the way down the trail, past the big teepee structure by the redwoods, past the Big X and the broken tree, past the Giant X and through the Aspen Grove, without pausing.

As they hurried along, they began to hear a crashing sound in the trees on both sides of the trail. It was like two very large animals, one on either side of them making as much noise as possible by shoving through the brush, breaking branches as they went, like they were noisily and rudely escorting Minnie, Musto and Dan out of the forest. The earth juddered with the sound of heavy weight stomping on both sides of the trail, accompanied by the wrenching of branches off trees and the snapping and tearing of saplings out of the ground.

'Run!' yelled Dan. They ran. The path through the trees joined the main hiking trail, and the cabins were just visible through the trees, when the thudding, shaking of the earth and crashing suddenly stopped. Minnie and Dan stopped too, and looked back. She opened her mouth to shout a last cheery farewell but before she could, the longest, loudest, deepest, roaring *h o o o w w l l l...* filled the very air they breathed, filled the air in the forest, filled the air over the bay, like twenty lions roaring together as one. But it was much, *much* louder!

The howl lasted many seconds then changed in tone until by the end it sounded like an anguished being crying out with anger, yearning and pride all in one giant voice. The howl echoed and faded away.

'OK then!' said Minnie to the forest.

'Er … wow,' said Dan in an awe-struck whisper, and they turned and walked quickly towards the cabins. Tears coursed down Minnie's freckled cheeks but she had the broadest smile on her face.

She was exhilarated, so fired with a quickening of joy and so aglow with wonder, that deep in her mind, a part of her asked if this was the summit of her life, if there could be more that would make her feel as alive as she felt at that moment. 'Thank you,' said Minnie to the sky. 'Thank you.'

Chapter Thirteen

Connie and Billy were standing on the deck of their cabin by the trail when Dan and Minnie came in sight through the trees. Connie ran down the steps when she saw them.

'Was that sound what I think it was? Minnie, where were you?' Connie ran to Minnie and swept her up in to her arms. 'When Dan said you hadn't slept in your bed...' Billy came over and joined in the hug.

Dan just stood looking up at the mountain, one trembling hand on his chest.

'It was like two trucks,' he said, gazing back at the trees, 'crashing straight down through the woods, but ... but ... with, like, you know, no engine noise...'

They all walked down to Connie's cabin, but kept looking back at the forest as they went, still wary, still shaken by the experience.

Connie took Minnie inside, leaving Billy and Dan on the deck, wrapped her in a blanket and fussed over her saying, 'Now, you must be starving. Are you starving? I'll make us all breakfast. Dan, you want coffee? Sit there, Minnie. Gosh, what is that on your head?'

Dan stepped inside the cabin. He checked that Billy wasn't right behind him. He could see the boy still stroking and cuddling Musto on the deck. He stood by Minnie at the sofa and said quietly to Connie, 'I don't want Billy to hear this but … Minnie fell and cut her head and her hand…' Minnie held up her hand '… and some … some how … when she woke up, this black resin stuff was on the cuts.'

Connie gasped. 'What?' She bent down to sniff Minnie's hand. 'There's a black pitch comes from the balsam tree. It's antispetic. But there's something green in there too, look.'

The three off them scrutinised the hard black crust. Connie looked at Dan. 'Could be juniper needles. Also antiseptic.' She stepped back. 'And there are fingerprints in it. Big fingers…' She leant against the table. 'OK, so … oh my!'

'And there were footprints again, all over.' Dan put his hands about eighteen inches apart. 'Like, yay big, again.'

Connie sat in the chair, and said, 'I can't hide this from Billy. He needs to know.'

They ate a hearty breakfast on the deck. French toast with maple syrup, scrambled eggs, bacon, tomatoes from the garden and steamed spinach, also from the garden, which Billy didn't eat but Minnie did.

'Gosh, you were ravenous,' said Connie. 'Now Dan, I hate to be crude and bring up business at the breakfast table, but wouldn't a Bigfoot encounter like this be good for business?'

'Encounter?' said Billy.

'I didn't see one,' corrected Minnie, 'but they've seen me.'

'They touched you,' said Connie firmly, 'so it's a *close* encounter. Look, there are fingerprints on that resin where they pressed it! Bigfoot fingerprints!'

'Big fingerprints,' contributed Billy, 'from a Bigfoot finger.'

'And they are not going to harm us, Billy', said Connie.

'It'll be just another report on a Bigfoot research organisation's website,' said Dan, 'and most people will simply say it didn't happen or say she put that stuff on herself, she'd hit her head … blah blah … she doesn't recollect correctly … blah blah…'

'Do you recollect correctly?' Billy smiled, relishing the word play. 'Or correctly recollect?' He employed the pepper grinder as a microphone, which he proffered in Minnie's direction and she started giggling with Billy.

'With that fire … no bookings…' Connie continued.

'With that fire they've had to move over this side of the mountain,' said Minnie, 'and so probably have other animals, like mountain lions.'

'And bears?' asked Billy.

'Or moose, bobcats, porcupines, coyotes…' said Minnie.

'Until that side grows back, which it will in a couple of years…' said Connie.

'Not the trees,' said Billy, 'they take way longer.'

'Decades,' said Minnie.

'Decades,' repeated Billy.

'I heard wolves,' said Dan.

'Wolves?' asked Billy.

'Not close. Far away,' Dan assured him. 'Far, far away.'

'Oh, and there was this.' Minnie pulled a long white strip of inner bark out of her jeans' pocket. 'I found this next to me when I woke up.'

They all just stared as Minnie chewed on the bark. 'It's yummy.'

Minnie took herself away from the others, went into her room and sat on her bed. She lifted the framed picture from the shelf – the one of her mom smiling while sitting on the jetty last summer on her birthday – held it to her chest and lay back on the bed.

'Onion!' She opened her backpack, pulled the wilted onion plants out and rolled off the bed. She ran out of the cabin and into the vegetable garden. After a brief hunt around she found striped green and yellow zucchini growing under their low spreading wide green leaves and twisted and hoiked four of them loose. Then she found the garlic and the parsley – she had to bite it to check it was parsley. Then she picked a nice pile of tomatoes. She lugged the vegetables back to the cabin in an old basket she found in the small tool shed, and set to making Dan's favourite meal.

It took her the rest of the morning and she was so exhausted after making the casserole and leaving it all ready to bake on the table with a cloth over it, that she went back to her bed to lie down. It was only then that she allowed herself to really think about what had happened in the forest.

She went over it in her head. 'While I slept, a Bigfoot crawled into my den and applied antiseptic goop to my cuts, then kept watch over me, chasing away a mountain lion?' She remembered how she fell down the ravine, slipping on the flat rocks, and how the next thing she knew she was up on the other side of the ravine, lying on her side with a leaf placed under her cheek. 'So he or she picked me up and carried me out of that ravine? And was watching me all that time?'

She remembered reading somewhere that some states in North America have signs up in the National Parks warning people to respect the local fauna *including* Sasquatch, which is the native name for Bigfoot.

She'd read on the internet that mostly they were believed to be fantasy beasts in stories told by First

Nations people to scare their kids and keep them from wandering off in to the woods. Which was exactly what Minnie had done.

She wondered why she hadn't been really scared in the woods, only anxious that Dan, Connie and Billy would realise she was missing and be worried. She wondered whether Bigfoots have extra special powers to sense the feelings of other animals and maybe they knew that she was sad about her mom, and maybe there was a Bigfoot rule not to harm any fauna that is sad. She thought about Dan, how he was sad and that the Bigfoots might know that too, and that Dan should let them into his thoughts and then he might have happy dreams about Mom.

She must have fallen asleep because she woke up to Dan tapping on her door. 'There's something on the table that looks particularly delicious.'

They ate together on the deck. 'Mmm … them's good eats!' said Dan, wiping his mouth. 'As good as, if not better than, your mom's.'

'A thank you for coming to get me this morning.'

'Well, thank *you*, Minnie.'

'And an apology for not doing as you said, not staying at Connie's.'

'Well, thank you, Minnie.'

'And an apology for saying the things I said to you before…'

'Well, again, thank you, Minnie.'

'When we were on the jetty, about me being a dreamer and Mom being a dreamer and you…'

'Yes, OK, well that's fine and I appreciate the gesture, Minnie. It was delicious.'

Minnie stood up and leant against the wooden rail that bordered the deck so she could look at the mountain stretching up behind their cabin.

'If you're thinking that you want to…' started Dan.

'No, I'm not thinking of going up Bigfoot Mountain any time soon, Dan, no.'

'You've given it a name?'

'Yup. It's a mountain, and there be Bigfoots, so…'

'Please keep that name to yourself.' Dan said, as he twisted the cap off a bottle of beer. 'Bigfoot Mountain? We need bookings!'

'There's plenty of Bigfoot researchers would love to come here,' said Minnie, 'Thing is, I don't want to share my Bigfoots with them, and my Bigfoots do not want to be bothered by people whacking trees, whoopin' and hollerin' at night in the woods and generally being a gosh darn nuisance. So I will be keeping this info to myself. And so will young Billy.'

'And so will I, Minnie,' said Dan.

'I think,' said Minnie, 'I think they deserve a bit of peace and quiet so I will not be going into that there forest, no Dan, not for a while. Even if I take Musto and Billy with me!'

'Billy? He's nearly as chicken as me!'

'You are not chicken, Dan, not when you've got your big gun to protect you. I reckon that's why they got close, Dan, because I had no gun. They're not stupid.'

'No, they're not,' he said.

'So you believe in Bigfoots now, Dan?'

'You mean there's more than one!' he laughed.

'There were at least three last night. We saw the moss they'd been sitting on,' said Minnie. Dan just smiled and looked away.

While they talked she picked at the hard black resin on her hand. 'If you don't believe they were Bigfoots watching over me? Who else was it? Hunters? Homeless people?'

'Let's not get in to this again,' he said.

'I know it's amazing and incredible, and blows your mind. It blows my mind too. But Dan, we saw the footprints. Huge! Hunters don't walk around barefoot in the forest at night. No one does, except… Oh. Look.'

She'd scraped the black resin crust off her cut hand and the two sides of the cut had knitted together, neatly and cleanly.

'That's … that's looking good. Should put a band aid on though so you don't open it up.'

'Yeah. I will.' Minnie said as she went in to the bathroom.

'I would leave the one on your head though, the resin … let it do its thing.'

Minnie came out with the first-aid box. She opened the box and Dan took out a sticking plaster, peeled the back off and stuck it over the cut.

'Thanks.'

'Wait,' he said, and he started to wind white bandage gauze round and round her hand and pinned it with a safety pin. 'I know how you love to climb your trees. That should hold.'

'Thanks, Dan.' She started stacking the plates. 'Can Billy and I go fish on the jetty? You can watch over us from the deck, like a king surveying his kingdom.'

Minnie leapt down the steps. Under the cabin was where they kept the fishing gear. She unhooked two rods and grabbed the tin of bait.

'Catch us something for tomorrow's lunch!' he yelled.

'We will!'

Chapter Fourteen

It was twilight, and day was fast fading to night. The waxing moon was cresting the hills in the southwest. The white cabins stood out, but everything else – the grass, the bushes, the paths – was lost in the murky gloom.

The tide was in. The water of the bay lapped and sloshed against the jetty posts under their dangling feet, as Minnie and Billy sat on the end with their fishing lines in the water. Neither of them had caught anything. 'So you weren't scared?' asked Billy.

'Yes and no! Sheesh! How many times you gonna ask me?'

'I would be, like, really scared, to be on my own in the forest,' said Billy.

'I know. You said. I had Musto with me,' said Minnie, 'and I just, kinda, fell asleep, without thinking about stuff too much. If I'd thought about it, I might have been more scared. OK? Happy? Can we not talk about it anymore?'

'Mom says I have an over-active imagination, and that it can stop me doing fun stuff. I just say I will do fun stuff, just not the dangerous fun stuff.'

'Walking in the forest is not dangerous,' said Minnie.

'If you carry a gun!' said Billy.

'No, Billy-Bug. If you take sensible precautions.'

'Like, stick to the hiking trails?' he said.

'Yes. But if you stick to the hiking trails you may not discover cool new stuff.'

'Like Bigfoots.'

'Right. But make sure you're back by nightfall…'

'So do you think they were there, looking after you,' asked Billy, 'like, all night?'

'I do, Billy, I do.'

'That is *so* cool! I hope you get some bookings for your cabins soon.'

'Why, Billy?'

'So I can scare their kids with stories of Bigfoot in the forest.'

'Don't do that, Billy. Do not do that. Or those people will not come back ever again. We need them to come back and to bring their friends! They won't do that if you're terrifying their children.'

'But it's true,' Billy said, as he pulled up his fishing line. 'There are Bigfoots in the forest.' His bait was gone.

'Billy, you must keep this information to yourself. Tell no one. Please, or we'll never get these cabins rented. Yes, they are in the forest.'

'But you haven't seen one.'

'No, I haven't *seen* one … but they will not bother you if you do not bother them. I went up too high, following Musto into their territory, and they didn't feel comfortable with that, so in the morning they let us know not to go that far up again. Up there,' she pointed up the mountain, 'is theirs. Down here is ours.'

'OK, I won't tell no one.' He was reeling in his line.

'That's a double negative, meaning you will tell someone. Are you being clever, young man?'

'I doubt it,' said Billy sincerely.

Clouds had floated in from the southwest, the sun had set, and night was closing in. Minnie wondered why Dan hadn't called her into the cabin. 'He must be engrossed in Bigfoot research,' she thought, as she could see him sitting on the deck with the laptop. While she was looking at him, she saw him answer his phone. Then he stood up and yelled, 'Minnie! Billy! Get up here now! Now!'

'What is it?' Minnie yelled as she pulled her line in.

'Run!' Dan was running down the path to the jetty with a desperate look on his face. 'Quickly! That was Connie. Something just thumped the side of her cabin, like twelve feet off the ground!'

BOOM!

'Like that?' said Minnie as something *thumped* hard on the back of their cabin. Dan grabbed Billy and Minnie and they all ran back up towards the cabin.

BOOM! Again.

They stopped and stared into the shadows.

'Let's go!' Dan led the way and they sprinted for the cabin. They ran up the steps, went inside and slammed the door shut. Dan went to the window on the side overlooking the vegetable garden and looked out. Billy grabbed Dan's arm. 'What's happening, Dan?'

'A Bigfoot just whacked the cabin,' said Minnie matter-of-factly. She was trying not to frighten Billy any more than he already was, by sounding

169

unemotional when in fact she was fizzing with excitement.

Dan went into the bathroom and Minnie followed him. Billy hurried after them. 'Why are we going in the bathroom?' he asked.

Dan peered out of the small window that was the only one at the back of the cabin facing the mountain and Connie's place.

'See anything?' Minnie asked.

'Nope.' Dan hurried out of the bathroom. He grabbed his torch off a shelf and his gun from its clips high on the wall and went out onto the deck. He turned on the torch. Minnie leant over the rail to look. The beam lit up a corner of the vegetable garden, the track up to Connie's and Connie's cabin. There was no movement, it was silent – no wind, no birds, and no barking from Musto. Nothing. Then a weird sound broke the silence – it was a warbling whistling sound, and it came from the trees behind Connie's cabin.

'What the…?' said Dan.

'That was like a whistle,' said Minnie, 'but with your lips loose and flapping.'

Dan pointed the strong beam of his torchlight in the direction of the whistle.

'Connie, stay there!' he yelled. 'I'm comin' to get ya!' He scanned the trees. Again, nothing stirred, nothing seemed out of place.

'What have you stirred up?' Dan said to Minnie.

'Me?' asked Minnie.

'Something's got them riled up.'

'They've had to move over to this side because of the fire!' she said.

'Why are they harassing us?'

'They're not!' she yelled.

'I'm gonna fire a warning shot to scare them back where they came from.'

'No, Dan, no. Leave them be! It may just be their way of saying hi!'

'Whacking the side of the cabin? It's aggressive behaviour! Go inside! I'm going to get Connie and lock the door!'

Dan sprinted off into the night, his torch beam jerking as he ran past the vegetable garden and through the parking area and round on to the track.

Minnie went inside. Billy was standing there, close to tears. 'Are they gonna come in?'

'No, they are not going to come in,' she said as she took his hand.

'What do they want?' he asked.

'They're just letting us know they are there.'

'Why? We already know they are there.'

'I'm not sure why. Dan's gone to get your mom. Look.'

She led him into the bathroom and from the window they could see the beam of light from the torch swinging this way and that, as Dan scanned the track, the trees and the cabin.

'They'll be back in a minute,' she assured him, 'less than a minute.'

As he passed behind the cabin Dan turned and directed the beam briefly on the back of the cabin and something caught Minnie's eye. Looking more closely she could see there were two handprints on the outside of the glass. The smaller handprint was much bigger than Minnie's hand and the bigger one was more than three times the size of her's with really long fingers. The prints were both slightly smeared, as if the hands that touched it had a sweaty, greasy sheen to them. Minnie and Billy both put their hands against the prints. She opened the window and yelled out, 'Dan!' but he must have gone inside Connie's cabin as the torch beam had disappeared.

'Just letting us know they're here?' Billy asked, weakly.

The torch beam reappeared. 'What? What is it, Minnie?' called Dan from outside Connie's.

'Look at this window.' Dan and Connie were running down the track, the torch beam jumping around ahead of them.

'Oh my!' said Connie, when they got up close. Dan reached his hand up to the window but the prints were about eight inches higher than he could reach.

Dan scanned with the torch all round, flicking the wide beam of light from bush to tree, to the trail up to the forest. 'Close the window. We're coming in.'

Minnie shut the window and locked it.

Dan and Connie came in and Billy rushed to his mother. Dan locked the door. They all stood there just looking at each other.

'OK, I think they've gone, so...' said Dan.

'Yes, they don't mean us any harm, let's just...' said Connie, still shaken, holding Billy who was hugging her tight.

'Let's see these prints, Minnie,' said Dan and they went in to the bathroom.

'Should we feed the kids, Dan?' called Connie.

'Yes, let's eat,' called Dan. 'There's zucchini casserole...'

Dan and Minnie looked closely at the prints. Dan snapped photos with his phone. Then he put his hand up and placed it over the bigger print. It was twice as long and twice as wide as Dan's hand.

'Er, what do you think?' asked Minnie.

'I don't know what to think,' Dan said, leaving the bathroom.

A short while later they were all sitting at the kitchen table, eating in a kind of shocked funk, as each of them tried to process what had happened. The adrenaline that had coursed through their bodies earlier had subsided, leaving them emotionally drained and physically weary. All the lights in the cabin were on and blazing brightly, casting a glowing pool of light around the cabin, in which the humans felt somewhat protected – like lighting a campfire in the woods to keep the beasts away.

'You can have my bed, Connie,' said Minnie.

'Minnie, thanks, but I'll be fine on the sofa, really.'

'How many nights are we staying?' asked Billy.

'Just as long as you want,' said Dan.

'No, no, just tonight.' said Connie, 'I'm still shook up about that thing hitting the side of my cabin. I was sitting right by that wall and boy, it made me jump! At first I thought it must have been a hiker, though there's been no one hiking since the fire started, that I've seen. Then I realised how high up that thing hit. Gotta be twelve feet off the ground at that point, maybe more.'

'And you're sure you didn't see the Bigfoots at the back of our cabin?' asked Minnie. 'The ones who touched the window?'

'I didn't move from the table until Dan got up there,' Connie said with a tremble in her voice.

'We don't know for sure it was Bigfoots,' said Dan.

'Er, hello?' said Minnie. 'The handprints?'

'OK, so, if it's them, why now?' asked Dan. 'There's been cabins here for fourteen years at least.'

'Must be the fire. Maybe they're competing for food now on this side,' said Minnie. 'That's why there's wolves, coyotes, mountain lion.'

'It'll be bears next. Just like the old days!' Connie refilled her glass from the water jug.

Minnie asked, 'Which cabins were built last?'

'Cabin number five was the last one your mom and I built, two years ago,' Dan said. 'But before that it was this one. Why?'

'Just wondering if maybe they want to get to the shore.'

'The shore?' said Billy.

'There's plenty of access up or down from here. From the rocks,' said Dan.

'But it's all slippy rocks, or cliffs. This is the only place with a beach at low tide,' said Minnie, 'so it's easy to access the water from here.'

'That's why there was always someone living here – access to the water,' said Connie.

'They can't get to the beach because of this cabin being in the way,' said Minnie, 'and they'd have to climb two high fences to get through the vegetable garden, or go all the way around the garden, and my tree, and through the parking area, through the gate…'

'So?'

'Well maybe they are like elephants, migrating elephants, who like to take the exact same route when they migrate.'

'Ha ha! Elephants!' Billy laughed.

'And this cabin is in the way,' added Minnie. 'Slap bang in the way.'

'But they're not migrating,' said Dan. 'Migration is seasonal, isn't it?'

Minnie pondered. 'Hmm…'

'Well, I'm flummoxed!' announced Billy.

'And I'm flabbergasted!' said Minnie and they laughed.

'Maybe they felt like seafood,' chimed in Connie. 'We all like a varied diet!'

'Yeah, Bigfoots can not live by strips of bark alone!' said Dan and they laughed again.

'Minnie, what do you think your mom would have made of all this?' asked Connie.

'She'd have loved it. She'd probably have been on the deck calling to them.'

'And throwing them bread!' said Billy. 'Like she did for the hawks and john crows.'

'And the golden eagles,' said Minnie, 'but they never took the bread because they…'

'They had bigger fish to fry,' said Dan, finishing the phrase with Minnie.

'As Georgie used to say!' said Connie. Dan stood up and looked straight out through the shut and locked glazed doors, into the darkness beyond the deck.

'Maybe I should put the jetty lights on,' he said.

'Did you hear something?' said Connie. 'I think I heard something.'

'Mom, please,' said Billy.

'No, I did really. I heard something.'

'What did it sound like?' asked Minnie.

'High-pitched call…' said Connie.

'So, a bird?' asked Billy, hopefully.

'Probably, honey.'

'Musto didn't hear anything, did you boy?' Billy bent down to stroke his dog, curled up under the table, snout nestled on his front paws, with his eyes open, ears twitching, listening to every sound, inside and outside. Dan picked up his rifle from where he'd stowed it on top of the cupboard.

'We're all a bit jumpy, I guess,' said Connie as she to bent to pat the worried-looking Musto.

Dan unlocked the doors, went outside, looked around with his torch and ran down the steps into the dark night. Minnie stood in the doorway looking out. She could see a movement on the jetty. She looked more closely. She could see that there was a bird, one *large* bird at the very end.

A moment later, and the four jetty lights secured

to the top of tall posts, snapped on, bathing the bottom of the property in a strong glow.

Now Minnie could see that the bird on the jetty was a golden eagle, and it was eating a fish. It took to the air a second after the lights came on, clutching the fish in its talons. Flapping its wings it flew quickly up and away out of the sphere of golden light.

Dan reappeared on the steps.

'Dan, I just saw a golden eagle on the jetty! Eating a fish!'

He looked down at the jetty. 'And we were just talking about them. Your mom's favourite bird, after hummingbirds and chickens!' They went back inside.

'Let's get that sofa bed out for you, Connie,' said Dan. 'See if we can get some sleep.'

'Billy, you want to sleep on the airbed in my room or out here with your mom?' asked Minnie.

Billy looked at his mother. 'Will you be OK on your own, Mom?'

She smiled, 'I think so, honey, and I will have Musto for company.'

So they pulled the airbed out of a cupboard and Minnie pumped it up with the foot pump, slid it against the wall, found clean sheets and blankets, had a brief pillow fight with Billy, and soon they were in their beds.

Dan came to the door. 'Will you two be alright? We'll all sleep with our doors open, shall we?'

'Yes!' said Billy.

'OK, goodnight, guys,' he said, as Connie came in.

She knelt down and held her son. She kissed him and said, 'We're safe here Billy, and I am quite sure they mean us no harm. They are being mischievous and playful and just, well, just saying hello.' She went over to Minnie and kissed her on the forehead. 'You, Minnie, are a brave, brave young adventurer. Your mom would be so proud of you.'

As she left she flicked out the light but left the door wide open.

'You wanna talk about the events of the last twenty-four hours anymore, Min?'

'Er, I'm all talked out, Billy-Bug.'

'Good. Me too,' said Billy yawning, 'but what do you think Bigfoots do all day?'

'Well, they are nocturnal mostly, so they sleep all day or just sit around eating snacks.'

'What, like, do they eat birds and squirrels?

'Mostly woodland snacks like berries, and lichen, and bits of grass and fern, and bugs. A handful of crickets is most nutritious!'

'Hmm … interesting,' murmured Billy drowsily.

As Minnie lay in bed she imagined that Billy, Connie and Dan were all doing the same as she was – listening for sounds outside that didn't fit with the usual pattern of night-time sounds in their tiny corner of the world, which tonight felt even more important, and even more special to her than it usually did.

Chapter Fifteen

Minnie woke in the morning to the sound of seagulls calling. She looked over at Billy who was still fast asleep. She could hear talking and quietly opened the door so as not to disturb Billy and crept out.

She smelt coffee. Minnie always thought, if she had to give a colour to a smell, coffee would definitely be brown. In the same way that cut grass smells green, but then she wondered if that was just because she knew the colour of those things.

She rubbed the sleep from her eyes as she entered the living room. Dan and Connie were sitting at the table looking out at the bay. They didn't see her.

'Look, Connie, I haven't *seen* any Bigfoots,' Dan was saying. 'I've seen footprints which I'm not sure about and the howl was pretty incredible, but…'

'And the *structures* you found, and the *pitch* on Minnie's wounds,' said Connie, 'and the *thumping* the cabins, *and* the handprints on the window, *and* being escorted out of the forest, Dan. Explain all *that*!'

'Minnie is still processing the loss of her mother, and finding these creatures, or imagining she is finding these creatures, is filling a void in her life.'

Minnie coughed and Dan and Connie looked round.

'You've got to stop eavesdropping on people, you know,' said Dan, surprised to see Minnie standing in the doorway to her room.

'You've got to stop talking about me!' said Minnie, and she hurried straight through the living room. 'I'm moving to South Bend, Indiana!' she called as she exited out the front door, barefoot in her blue pyjamas, slamming the door shut after her, and hurrying down the steps.

She expected Dan to come out and yell at her but he didn't. She kept on walking down the path towards the jetty. She could feel the blood reddening her face – she was so upset and frustrated – she *knew* Bigfoots existed, she just *knew* it! She didn't want to leave this place. She wanted to find out more about the extraordinary beings living on the forested slopes behind her. That's what she wanted to do. She felt like her mom wanted her to do that too. She'd loved this place so much. If she'd known about the Bigfoots, what would she have done? She'd have embraced them, maybe not literally but…

These thoughts and others tumbled through her head as she walked down the slope. The sun was already warming the grassy path, the sky was pale sapphire blue, and a whispering breeze tickled the tops of the trees and rippled the watery bay. Seagulls circled and called above the jetty, and it looked like it was going to be another beautiful summer day.

At the end of the path there were three steps down to the wooden planking, and what she saw there on the jetty made her stop in her tracks.

KAAYII

Chapter Seven

Kaayii was flying over water. He had feathery brown wings and in his bright yellow talons he clutched two green pinecones. Gliding over the long, hilly, tree-covered island across the bay, he dropped the pinecones near where the lightning strike had left scorched blackened trees.

Ahniiq was prodding him with a stick. Rudely awakened, Kaayii just looked at him, asking: *why?* Then he heard the girl calling out the small yellow dog's name, 'Musto'. He and his uncle were lying by a fallen redwood tree trunk, under a pile of brown leaves and branches. Parting the tall grass in front of them, they could see the tree where the girl had slept.

The crow was perched nearby. Shiny black wings flapped, it lifted and flew away. The two Sasquatches smiled broadly as they watched the small human girl crawl out from under the tree and look around with a confused expression on her funny, freckled face.

Two things happened in quick succession- a tree knock – *klunk* – rang out from not far away up the mountain. Then they heard a dog barking excitedly, approaching from down the mountain.

They watched, fascinated, as the girl quickly climbed a tree. She jumped up and grabbed a branch with her hands and then lifted up her legs and hooked her feet over the branch and somehow twisted and pulled until she was sitting on the sturdy limb. She climbed higher. Sasquatches are so strong they can pull themselves up by their arms alone. *Good climber,* Kaayii thought.

The dog bounded through the trees and a man's voice shouted in the woods below. The girl shouted something back. The same man as before appeared, struggling up the short steep slope. Kaayii felt sure he was not her father, and he could sense a desperate fear attached to him. He was carrying a killing stick, and seeing it his uncle put his hand on Kaayii's arm. They eased down slightly lower in the undergrowth. When the man reached the girl, he embraced her, and Kaayii sensed that most, but not all, of the man's fear had subsided.

Kaayii and Ahniiq started crawling through the undergrowth from bush to tree to long grass, so they could see and hear better. That's what Kaayii thought they were crawling closer for, but then Ahniiq raised himself up to kneeling and hurled a pinecone at the man. It missed, but only just.

Kaayii sniffed the ground and caught the unmistakable scent of fungi in the air. His long black fingers with their black nails searched the ground, pulling at the moss and grass, finding a clump of small golden mushrooms. He nudged his uncle. Ahniiq reached his open hand over so Kaayii could drop some of the egg yolk-yellow fungi with orange-tinted stems in his black leathery palm, and they ate the mushrooms greedily. The firm flesh was delicious – nutty, tangy and creamy.

Kaayii sensed the presence of his father Taashi nearby. From the underbrush on the far side of the group of pine trees where the girl and the man were now crouched down, looking at the earth, trying to identify animal tracks, his father must have thrown a pinecone because Kaayii saw one fly through the air and nearly hit the girl. The two humans started hurriedly walking away down the mountain.

As they walked away the girl was calling out to the forest, or to Kaayii – she was looking in his direction. He sensed strong feelings of joy and gratitude from her, and he could see again that faint shimmer of special energy she had all around her.

His uncle set off down the slope through the heavy brush, intentionally stepping with all his weight, each step a heavy THUD! They could hear Taashi on the other side of the retreating humans, deep in the brush, doing the same – intentionally walking with a heavy tread. The three Sasquatches kept out of sight but made a lot of noise by pushing through bushes and branches as they crashed through the forest parallel to the humans and the dog.

It was fun to smash through the underbrush without a care for all the noise they were making and Kaayii had to restrain himself from whooping with sheer delight.

They ripped down branches and they snapped saplings. They stomped heavily and Kaayii could feel the ground juddering. They kept pace with the man and girl the whole way down the mountain, which wasn't hard as humans move slowly.

When the bay came into view through the trees and the people's gathering place was in sight, the three Sasquatches stopped breaking branches, and crouched down and watched. The man and the girl were greeted by the small boy and a woman. Kaayii felt this woman was not the girl's mother. He wondered where the girl's parents were and thought maybe the deep sorrow he'd sensed in her the first time he'd seen her was because her parents had passed to the next life.

His uncle then howled a territorial howl, one of the extra long and loud ones that tells other Sasquatches that this is their mountain and theirs only. It was meant to signal that Kaayii's clan hunted, fed and lived there, so 'Keep Out', unless the intention was to make friends or honour the passing of a clan member. Kaayii watched the human girl as she looked back up at the forest and he felt sure she would be drawn to the wooded slopes again, howl or no howl.

Hidden in the dense evergreen brush under the trees looking down the trail, the three Sasquatches could see the cabins directly in front of them, and beyond those they could see and smell the bay. Small waves were capping in a strengthening breeze, and across the water, bathed by a gap in the cloud cover in a blaze of sunshine, lay the green, tree-covered, hump-backed island.

Taashi nudged his son with an elbow and pointed at the island across the glittering grey water.

Chapter Eight

The three Sasquatches walked back up the mountain. Kaayii was leading them to the honey he'd found in the oak tree and as they passed silently through the woods his father dropped back with Ahniiq to talk with him. When Kaayii reached the oak tree, he waited for them.

His uncle's eyes were clouded with worry. His father was still talking and the words he chose meant, 'After the fire too many animals are here. Teach the wolves to take enough and no more.'

As Kaayii climbed up to the hollow in the tree, to the bees' nest, the bees buzzed about him agitatedly and crawled over the long, dark brown hairs of his arms. He flicked them away, and reached down with handfuls of sticky, golden honeycomb.

'I do not want to be guardian of the forest!' Ahniiq answered through a mouth full of honey, 'There are no caves on this side of the mountain!'

'You will find one,' Taashi assured him. 'Talk to the animals. They can help.'

'I am not good with animals.'

'Spend time with Kaayii. He knows the ways of the animals. He was gifted by his forefathers when he was born.'

'I know,' murmured Ahniiq. 'We all know.'

Kaayii dropped down from the tree and they continued in an uneasy silence up the mountain, gorging on their honey, until his father silently reminded Kaayii: *you are day watcher*.

His father and his uncle both touched his head with the palm of a hand affectionately and left him alone by a juniper bush, as they walked on up the slope towards the first ravine. Kaayii turned and, still licking the honey from his fingers, strolled down through the woods in the direction of the Watcher's Place.

As he moved through the trees, he began to sense animal energy nearby. His awareness heightened, he listened with his whole being to the forest. Ahead, squirrels were chattering loudly.

Kaayii found a good, strong stick as thick as his wrist and quickened his pace. Approaching the Watcher's Place, squirrels were chattering noisily. The crow landed nearby and communicated one thought: *wolf*.

Treading stealthily closer, he became aware that a wolf, and it looked like the same wolf from before, was *sitting* in the hollow of the Watcher's Place, looking out across the bay.

Kaayii growled in anger – it was a growl that turned in to a howl that turned into a high-pitched scream. It got the wolf's attention. Kaayii was pleasantly surprised by his growl-howl-roar as he hadn't done one before. He considered letting rip with another, but thought it might bring other Sasquatches to investigate and he didn't need them – this was a situation he needed to handle himself.

It was indeed the same big, stocky wolf, black but with brown chest markings and those same staring yellow eyes. To Kaayii's surprise the wolf communicated a thought: *follow*, then jumped out of the Watcher's Place, and trotted away from him without looking back.

Clutching the stout stick, Kaayii ran leaping and bounding over branches and fallen trees, cutting through chest-high pale grass, meaning to catch up with the wolf quickly and to teach it a lesson for sitting uninvited in the Watcher's Place. The wolf's long loping stride was deceptively effective and it took some effort for Kaayii to catch up, as the wolf could run straight through and under brush that Kaayii had to go around.

Running after the wolf lifted his spirits. The feeling of the wind rushing through the long hairs on his arms and legs was exhilarating – he felt a vital connection to the living, breathing, throbbing heart of his forest home, and it delighted him.

He caught up with the wolf, and they ran together, Kaayii a few strides behind him. He forgot about teaching him a lesson and instead tuned in to the wolf's energy. He was curious about why the wolf had wanted him to follow.

They came to some patches of mud left by a stream that had dried up between the all-too-brief spells of summer rain. This was not a part of the forest that Kaayii had visited before and he was wary. There was water pooling in the mud and the wolf lapped at it with his pink tongue. Kaayii knelt down and drank with him.

Kaayii had never been this close to a wolf before and thought he'd try something. He made a short clear sound, 'Huff!' The wolf turned and looked at him. So Kaayii stood and walked a few paces away from the pond and without looking back made the same sound, 'Huff!' The wolf trotted to his side and gazed up at him.

Tracks led through the mud: of deer and of mountain lion, and the much smaller tracks of squirrels, weasels and martens. The wolf fixed his gaze on a high bluff, steep and dark, tinted with layers of grey and topped with reddish rocks rounded and smoothed by millions of years of weather.

As they ran up the dry streambed, they passed the muddy remains of a shallow pond, criss-crossed by more animal tracks. The forest became less dense until the only trees were occasional pines. On they ran, through grasses, bleached pale as straw by the summer sun, and low-growing yellow flowers, amongst dark, spiky bushes.

At the base of a steep outcrop of rock shouldering out of the face of the mountain was a thicket of bare oak trees, and tall spruce pines strung with dead creepers looping down from the cliff above. Kaayii glanced at the wolf and looked to where he was staring. At the base of the pines, under the lowest of their branches he could now make out faces, and they were all looking at him.

Chapter Nine

Kaayii and his new wolf friend Huff stopped about two throws away from the pines, and slowly the wolf pack emerged. There were ten of them, mostly black but some a dark muddy brown. All were stocky, with shiny coats and clearly well fed. Huff nudged Kaayii's leg with his black snout. Kaayii took a step forward. The wolf nudged him again. Kaayii stepped forward again.

Kaayii tuned in to the scents wafting around, carried by the swirling breeze that was rocking the tops of the trees as it gusted off the high grey rocks. He could detect the scent of pine, of wolf, of mud, flowers and fresh *blood*. Now he could see that some of the wolves, the bigger ones, had blood around their mouths, showing deep red on their black furry muzzles.

The feeling he got from the wolves was an alert curiosity, but not aggression and not fear. They were simply waiting to resume feeding. Within a moment the energy changed. The interlocking low green boughs of two spruce trees twitched and moved and parted. Pushing through them into the open came the largest wolf Kaayii had ever seen.

This wolf's whole head was smeared, and his muzzle washed to the eyes, in warm blood. It dribbled from his jaws. He was twice the size of the smaller wolves, and bulging bunched muscles made the black fur ripple at his rolling shoulders as he walked. He halted in his advance, looked at Kaayii and bared his yellow teeth. Kaayii's wolf nudged him on the leg again and communicated one thought to the young Sasquatch: *fight him*. Kaayii looked down at the wolf and communicated one simple thought back to him: *no!*

A young female, black but for one of her ears which was light brown, took a few steps towards Kaayii and Huff. Immediately the giant wolf ran and barrelled into her, knocking her to the ground, chomping on her ear. She yelped, scrabbled to her feet, and with her tail between her legs hurried back to her place in the pack.

Keeping his eyes fixed on the leader, Kaayii paced sideways, curious to see what was behind the trees. Between and behind two spruces the tall grass had been flattened and covered in blood from a kill. Sticking up from the ground, amongst the grass and low scrub he could see the remains of several deer, and could just make out the wide flat antlers of a moose. So big were the antlers that they must have been from a bull moose. He peered at them, studying the arrangement of the antler points, and something deep in Kaayii darkened.

The pack leader advanced a few paces towards Kaayii, baring his teeth and snarling aggressively. The rest of the pack advanced, and he knew he had to fight or run. Then he had an idea – from deep in his throat, he began to hum one long, low note. The wolves were creeping closer. He opened his throat, finding an even lower note, using his chest space so the sound rumbled more. The wolves kept coming. He took another deep breath and tried again, making an even deeper rumbling *hum*, and the wolves stopped, whimpered and backed away, except the big alpha male who kept advancing.

Kaayii bent down to his wolf companion, grabbed his ears, looked in to his yellow eyes: *follow me*. And that was when the giant wolf leapt. Its massive paws struck Kaayii hard on the shoulder and he hit the ground hard. Huff jumped at the wolf but not before it had snapped its jaws shut on Kaayii's ear. Both wolves tumbled away from the Sasquatch, gnashing, growling, biting, and rolling. Kaayii grabbed the wolf by the scruff of its neck, lifting it off Huff, and hurled it into a spiky thorn bush.

Kaayii and Huff ran.

The sun was high and the wind sent a whisper through the tall grass as Kaayii and his wolf friend stood at the edge of the Sasquatch gathering place on the High Ridge. His ear, now with a V-shaped notch in it, had stopped bleeding but there was blood on his shoulder and chest. Behind them to the north, smoke rose in twisting ribbons and curtains of grey over the smouldering, charred, black slopes.

Amongst the pines near the clearing, Kaayii's mother and his little sister Yaluqwa sat on the vast trunk of the fallen redwood and watched as eight Sasquatches silently and solemnly walked out of the clearing and stood together under the pines. There, looking down into the forest, were Kaayii, Taashi, Ahniiq, the other pair Ahnoosh and

Yaaqwun, and their daughter Shumsha, and the older pair Wesh and Enksi.

Nothing felt out of place on the wooded slopes, so Taashi, Kaayii, and Huff the wolf, hurried down the game trail between the trees. Then two more Sasquatches left the stand of pines heading down the trail and, in pairs, they hurried down from the ridge and quickly melted into the dense forest.

As they traversed the tree-clad inclines at a steady jog, the crow flew along with them. Squirrels called excitedly, sensing something was afoot, and ground dwellers like raccoons, polecats, porcupines and possums lay low as the earth trembled with the passing of the giant running beings.

Hefty sticks were snatched up from the forest floor as they progressed through the trees and underbrush, and when they arrived at the dried-up stream Taashi raised his stick and the Sasquatches stopped and gathered round.

The water of the stream, when it was running, had eroded the ground and exposed grey rocks, and Taashi crouched down in the streambed and rubbed mud and dirt from a half-buried rock. It was quartz. He placed one vast hairy black hand on the glistening quartz and Kaayii took hold of his other hand. The other Sasquatches dropped their sticks and grouped together. The last Sasquatch in the chain, Ahniiq, crouched down and placed his hand on the quartz next to Taashi. They all closed their eyes and felt the energy from the earth pulsing through the forest, and through them.

A few moments later the crow called a warning. Kaayii led the group up the path by the streambed. The crow alighted on the branch of a pine by the dried-up pond, where the path opened up into the clearing of pale grass, yellow flowers and spiky bushes. The grey, rocky bluff towered above them. The Sasquatches advanced slowly on the stand of spruces at the base of the cliff.

Kaayii could not feel the presence of wolf but their senses were heightened and they approached with great care: silently, stealthily.

Taashi looked down at the wolf, Huff, close to Kaayii's side and asked: *where?* Huff glanced at the Sasquatch and, trotting forward a few paces, sniffed the air. The wolf looked up at the high rocky bluff.

Behind the spruces were the remains of the bull

moose – his head, antlers and feet. There were also carcasses of four white-tailed deer amongst the bloody, flattened grass. Taashi stood over the body of his friend the moose and the words he solemnly uttered meant, 'It was not yet the time for my friend to pass.'

Huff sniffed a deer carcass and pulled some meat off a leg with his front teeth. He trotted off with the meat, and Kaayii followed him down a thin path snaking through huge boulders to the base of the cliff. Huff disappeared behind the boulders into a dark and narrow space. Kaayii followed. The wolf barked. It was a friendly bark, not a warning, so Kaayii twisted his body and squeezed in. Kaayii shouted, 'Oosh!' and his voice echoed in the deep, dark opening under the cliff.

Three Sasquatches leaned their backs against the boulder and heaved until it shifted a few inches. They heaved again. Ahniiq and Taashi could now squeeze into the gap and they disappeared into the gloom.

Kaayii and the others waited among the

boulders, watching warily for the return of the wolves, sticks in hand. Huff turned his head towards the rocky slope and the hackles on the back of his neck stood up. Kaayii noticed and stepped to the wolf's side, scanning the slope for any movement.

Moments later the brothers came out of the cave into the daylight, and Ahniiq was rubbing the top of his head. Taashi looked at Kaayii: *this cave is too small.*

Caw caw! Called the crow. The Sasquatches hurried through the boulders back to the feeding place, where the wolf pack could now be seen scrambling down the rock-strewn stony slope, with the massive alpha male leading them.

The wolves gathered on the bloody grass, the dominant male standing firm, facing the Sasquatches. He stepped forward, correctly identifying Taashi as their leader, looking directly into his black eyes, and lowering his head in wary challenge.

Ahniiq pointed with his club at the carcasses: *you killed too many.*

'Wha! Whaa!' barked Taashi, raising his club, but the wolves did not go, they did not move a muscle, they stood staring with piercing yellow eyes, alert and ready. The giant male took another step forward, glancing back at the ten in his pack. None advanced with him, and two looked away, down at the ground. But the proud male, primed for action, took another step towards the Sasquatch who stood almost three times the height of the wolf's shoulders.

Taashi launched himself at the wolf, taking two quick short steps and springing through the air at him whilst swinging the club, which connected with the wolf's shoulder as it ducked and sprang sideways.

'Wha!' he yelled again at the wolf, but it growled through its teeth, snarling aggressively. The pack advanced on Taashi baring their fangs, and instantly the other Sasquatches rushed at the ten wolves swinging their solid lengths of wood and in a split second all the wolves recoiled as one and fled, spraying blood and grass underfoot as they scrabbled for purchase on the wet, sticky ground.

Now the giant wolf was angry and bared hellishly sharp-looking yellow fangs and jagged teeth. He rushed at Taashi, sinking his teeth into his thigh even as the Sasquatch pounded his club on the beast's black skull. Kaayii threw himself at the wolf, wrapping both his arms around its body with enough force to make the wolf release his grip on his father's leg.

With the other wolves having retreated to a safe distance, Ahniiq also jumped on to the black wolf's back. Subdued by the two Sasquatches the wolf lay on its side, eyes and snarling jaws furiously contorted by the indignity of being pinned down and having his muzzle shoved into the bloodstained mud. Taashi knelt down and grabbed it by the throat. Squeezing hard he growled at the brute, right in its ear...

They released the wolf and it ran to join the others in the pack. The Sasquatches ran after it, spreading out, with arms held wide, forming a semi-circle around the wolves, herding them up the rocky slope beside the grey cliff.

A lone female wolf peeled away from the pack, doubling back. Huff galloped after her. The brown-eared wolf slowed her pace when she saw Huff following her and circling round a small boulder she stopped as he came to her side. They sniffed each other.

The rest of the wolf pack crested the ridge at the

top of the bluff, closely followed by the Sasquatches. The wolves scampered down the loose grey shale, now in shadow, beyond which the scorched forest lay dark and desolate. At the bottom of the slope the big alpha male stopped and looked back up at the crest where the Sasquatches stood together, silhouetted against the day's last glow, eight towering, gargantuan figures. The wolf turned and trotted away.

Chapter Ten

It was almost dark by the time Kaayii, his father and his uncle left Huff and his new she-wolf friend sitting in the Watcher's Place.

The three Sasquatches reached the first cabin on the trail down from the mountain as night closed in. They could sense a human energy inside the cabin. It was thrilling to Kaayii to be so close to the humans' homes and he felt a rush of excitement course through his body.

Taashi crept down the side of the cabin listening intently. He peeped round the corner of the building. There was nothing on the deck, no humans in sight. He signalled to the other two. They trod softly, carefully. Straight ahead was the other cabin, with a rocky outcrop close to one side and a high fence on the other.

Kaayii's father pointed at the one window on the rear of the cabin facing them. He and Kaayii reached up and placed their flat palms and fingers on the glass. It felt like nothing they'd ever felt before – smooth, but hard and cold, like ice. Taashi grunted angrily, and his words meant, 'People are on our ancient trail!'

Ahniiq was by the fence smelling the odours from the plants there. Some were new smells, strange and pungent, whilst some were fruity, some earthy, some like nothing he'd ever smelt. The fence came up to Kaayii's face. Ahniiq put his hands on the top of the fence. He realised it was not strong enough to hold his weight.

Taashi walked away from the fence back up the track in to the shadows mumbling gruffly to himself.

Kaayii and Ahniiq watched him go. When Taashi passed the first cabin he whacked the side of it really hard with the flat of his hand, BOOM! It was so loud that Kaayii and Ahniiq quickly stepped into the shadows of the underbrush under the rocky outcrop.

More lights went on in the second cabin. They could just about hear a human talking inside it. They stepped out of the shadows and Ahniiq whacked the back of the cabin right near where they were standing, BOOM! Then Kaayii stepped from the shadows grinning mischievously, and he too whacked the back of the cabin, BOOM!

They waited. They heard shouting and his uncle pulled Kaayii by the arm, yanking him back into the shadows of the underbrush.

A light came on inside casting a block of light from the small back window onto the dusty track. Slowly the window opened and the man looked out. He was so close that Kaayii could have lobbed a pinecone in through the opening. The man closed the window and the light inside went off.

Moments later a bright light was shone up the side of the cabin onto the fence and the cabin beyond.

A 'warble-whistle' rang out. Kaayii knew this kind of whistle meant 'let's go' and it had come from his father in the trees. Ahniiq looked at Kaayii: *I want fish.*

Beyond the cabin the strong white light reappeared and started jerking around, sweeping the ground and flashing up into the trees. The man shouted something. He was carrying the light and was coming round the big pine tree onto the track towards them.

They crouched low in the shadows and though the light swept over them the man kept going. He stopped and turned the light back onto the cabin, light flooding the back of the building. Then he turned and hurried up the track to the other cabin up the slope.

The light went on again inside the small window and they saw two very small hands pressed against the inside of the glass.

Ahniiq nudged Kaayii: *squirrels?*

The man and a woman appeared, hurrying down the steps of the first cabin and running down the track, with the torchlight jerking around ahead of them. The window opened and the girl yelled out. The man and the woman stopped just a few feet from Kaayii and Ahniiq, and looked at the handprints. Ahniiq started giggling and Kaayii had to nudge him hard in the arm to shut him up. The man and the woman ran on and the window closed.

His uncle stood up and left the shadow of the underbrush. Kaayii grabbed a branch off the ground and quickly swept away any sign of footprints in the dust. He followed his uncle.

Ahniiq led him up the outcrop climbing a steep tumble of boulders. At the top of the cliff there was a tall, thin stick with what looked like four white seagulls' wings on top, slowly turning in the wind.

Kaayii sniffed the sea breeze and was reminded of the salty scent deep in the yellow wolf's coat.

They looked down on the cabins dotted about the grassy slope. They clambered down the steep path scattered with loose small rocks leading to the shore and struggled to climb safely down the jagged tumble of slippery grey boulders in the dark.

The tide was still in and they lowered themselves into the water. Kaayii gasped with shock at the sudden coldness. It came up to Kaayii's waist and they waded out holding hands, feeling the rocks, large and small, embedded in the sand and the slippery seaweed underfoot.

Kaayii watched as his uncle stood still in the gentle swell, with both his long arms hanging in front of him. He copied Ahniiq and they stood there, motionless, waiting with their hands in the water. Kaayii could sense his uncle sending a calm energy through the water.

Moonlight glittered in the silvery *splash* made by Ahniiq whipping his hands up out of the water, clutching a wriggling, gleaming fish with whisker-like barbells protruding from beneath its mouth. Ahniiq promptly started to eat the fish.

Kaayii waded along the shore, where seaweed

draped the rocks and swayed in the shallow swell of the sea. He glanced back to see Ahniiq pulling a handful of seaweed out of the water and biting in to it. Kaayii did the same – the seaweed was salty, slimy and delicious.

He stood waist high in the water near the end of the jetty, put his hands under the surface and sent calm energy out into the shifting watery blackness. He heard an eagle's high-pitched cry above him just as a fish tickled his fingers. He seized it with both hands and in one motion pulled up and flung the fish onto the end of the wooden jetty.

Circling above him was the eagle, which at that moment swooped low. It brushed the top of Kaayii's head with its talons and, lowering its huge wings, braked in the air to drop expertly and land softly on the jetty. The eagle's cry of thanks pierced the stillness. The bird grasped the flapping fish and began to feed.

Suddenly a bright golden light burst from high posts by the jetty startling Kaayii. He ducked down into the perfect black shadow under the jetty, the water up to his neck. The eagle kept feeding and Kaayii's uncle did the same, sitting on a rock, and watching the spectacle of the eagle feeding on the jetty while Kaayii hid below in the watery shadows. Then the eagle flapped his huge wings, and lifted up, still holding the fish, and disappeared into the night sky.

Keeping low in the water, Kaayii could see the girl and the man silhouetted by the light from the cabin. The man had his killing stick. Soon they went back inside and closed the door. Kaayii stared up at the cabin and thought about how they had hit the back of their home, and how it must have worried them. He decided he wouldn't hit their home again.

He waded back across to his uncle who was eating another fish, and making noises as he ate that reminded Kaayii of feeding coyotes – a kind of grunting, gasping, spluttering noise.

Ahniiq flicked away the bare backbone and tail, and swam out into deeper water, the long hairs of his shoulders, back and arms trailing behind him. Kaayii followed him. His uncle dived down into the inky black sea. Kaayii waited … and waited … until Ahniiq's huge black conical head broke the surface, emerging triumphant with oysters in his hands and a broad smile on his face. His yellow teeth had bits of seaweed stuck in them and soon they would have shell stuck in them too as he crunched through an oyster shell and sucked out the animal. He dropped the shattered shell, and crunched into another.

Kaayii dived down into the depths. The sound of bubbling and swooshing water and the thrumming of the blood in his ears reminded him of the sounds that trees make in springtime, when water is moving up from the earth, up through the trunk to the crown of the tree.

He searched with his hands among the seaweed and, feeling something hard and round, he pulled. It came away and he kicked and kicked, looking up through the water to the sky – a ghostly grey promise beyond the invisible skin of the sea. In his hand he held a mussel, wedge-shaped, smooth and midnight blue.

Pleased with himself, Kaayii swam back to the shore where Ahniiq had climbed onto the rocks and up the steep path. He whistle-warbled from the top of the rocky climb, but Kaayii waved him away – he had something important to do right there at the shore. He knew the human girl would understand the feeling behind his actions, but he also knew the human man with the killing stick would not.

MINNIE

Chapter Sixteen

As Minnie stepped on to the jetty three seagulls flew away. Across the full width of the jetty, artfully arranged in a circle, were shellfish – dark-blue mussels, small grey limpets, white cockles, silver and black striped oysters, pink scallops and brown clams. Forming a cross perfectly dividing the circle into four quarters were strips of green and brown seaweed. Laid on top of the seaweed were fish – two silver-grey salmon and two grey-green cod. In the centre of the design was a large red spiny sea anemone.

The seagulls had attacked some of the oysters and eaten parts of the fish, but the circle was was beautiful. It was staggering to Minnie because she felt she knew who had put it there. She knew who had taken the time to find these creatures – to swim and to dive, to probe amongst the rocks as the tide went out and to arrange them.

'Dan!' she yelled. 'Connie!'

The three of them stood and gawped. Dan knelt down to look under the jetty. The tide was coming in again, and the only activity on the exposed shore was a wading seabird stalking the mudflats, exposed by the receding tide.

Dan snapped photos with his phone. 'I turned the lights off about midnight to save power. I'm sure there was nothing then.' Musto sniffed the fish then turned and trotted back along the jetty. He jumped down on the rock and entered the water, swimming round and round in circles.

'Maybe they left footprints down there.' Minnie started to climb down the side of the jetty to the muddy strip of beach and rocks.

'The tide has come in and out, Minnie,' said Connie.

'This is not good,' said Dan.

'Oh my gosh!' said Connie, gazing at the circle.

'What is it?' asked Dan.

'Is it lined up like a compass? That fish is pointing due west, look.' Connie pointed at the fish and lifted her arm to point due west across the bay towards the big long island where the sun sets. 'And that one is exactly north…'

'Well, that proves this was not Bigfoots,' said Dan, 'so that's good, in a way.'

'That is so cool,' said Minnie, ignoring Dan. 'This is a gift. They are saying sorry for frightening us with the banging on the cabins.'

'That's ridiculous,' said Dan.

'No, Dan, it is not,' said Connie. 'I think Minnie is right.' She turned and looked up at the mountain.

'So why did they bang on the cabins?' said Dan.

'They want access to the shore,' Minnie said as she prowled the strip of beach, where waves were gently lapping on the round grey rocks. 'Musto! What are you doing? Here, boy!' Musto swam towards her. Emerging from the water, he ran to Minnie, shook the seawater off his coat and licked her hands. 'Can you still smell our visitor, Musto?' She patted and fussed him and pulled up his ears.

Pointing at the seafood circle Dan said, 'They *have* access to the shore! Look!'

'I think this is just one or two of them, if there'd been more, we'd have heard them,' Minnie called.

'Or was it you, Connie?' asked Dan. Connie and Minnie laughed at the suggestion.

'You think I'd leave this beautiful seafood harvest out here for the gulls?'

'This would take all night to catch,' said Minnie. 'Good job, Connie!'

'OK, OK,' said Dan. 'So, Minnie, you think they whacked the cabins because we're in their way? They've never whacked the cabins before.'

'It's the fire,' she said. 'There's less food because there's more competition on this side of the mountain now. Either that or they just want to be able to go for a swim on warm nights without carrying their towels and their picnic stuff over those big slippy rocks!' She and Connie laughed, Dan didn't – he just gazed at the sea life arranged on the jetty.

Billy had emerged from the cabin and was standing on the deck. 'Hey, what's so darn funny?'

They sat on the deck around the table sorting and cleaning the big bowl of seafood. 'Won't they be upset that we left the fish down there?' asked Billy.

The gulls were still picking at the fish down on the jetty. 'The gulls had already gorged on the fish,' said Connie. 'We have plenty here.'

Dan took a sip of his coffee and said, 'I think it's time we moved.'

'What? No!' said Minnie. 'No, Dan! No!'

'Wait. Listen, I'm not saying I'm a Bigfoot believer but maybe we should think about moving this cabin. Maybe to just there, backed up against the cliff.' He pointed to the small cliff with the wind turbine on top of it. 'We could make it bigger, and two levels so I can walk out the back and check the turbine without having to climb up that cliff.'

Minnie jumped up from the table and hugged Dan, spilling his coffee. 'Thank you! Thank you, Dan!'

'OK,' said Dan, 'so when do we start?'

Minnie grinned. 'Right now.'

Chapter Seventeen

It took them the rest of that day to move all their stuff over to cabin number one, the closest cabin, with the help of Connie and Billy. By the end of the day, placed all around on the grass were things they couldn't fit in, like the fridge, the cooker, desks, lamps, small tables, and their beds. Dan spread a big green tarp over most of it, though it didn't look like it was going to rain any time soon.

The next day he removed the roof in three sections, and by the end of day three he had dismantled the walls by unscrewing each wooden plank that had been stacked and attached to the frame.

Then he started removing the floorboards, so by midday on day four all that remained of their cabin was eight, fat, cobwebby posts sticking out of the ground, surrounded by what had been the dusty, flat-earth floor under the cabin, where they'd stored bikes, tools, a lawn mower and other family stuff in sturdy plastic boxes.

Now that the cabin was gone you could walk up the path from the jetty, through the eight big posts by the vegetable garden, and on to the hiking trail, straight up to the mountain.

'Hey, Minnie, what say we have a wrap-around deck,' Dan called, dumping the last floorboard in the pile, 'on all three sides. That way there's nothing for your Bigfoot to whack. I'll build the back wall right up against the cliff face. Yeah? Like it?'

He was grinning at her and she gave him a thumbs-up. This new project seemed to have energised Dan. She had never seen him work so hard, and he'd even started whistling while he worked. She hadn't heard him whistle for a long time.

Minnie remembered when she was little a new cabin appeared most summers, but a few years ago her mom had needed help to build *two* new cabins – numbers four and five on the little rocky rise over on the far side. She'd asked around town for recommendations. The only construction company based in the town couldn't help as they were building a fancy new fishing lodge down in the south part of the bay.

Dan had showed up one day with a truckload of

tools and he had never really left. He and her mom had built the cabins together, and Minnie didn't know it at the time but that cacophony of hammering and sawing, accompanied by whistling and laughter, was the soundtrack to the most important love story in her mother's life.

Dan was looking through the stuff in one of the boxes as Minnie lay in the sun with Musto on the grass nearby.

'Hey Minnie, you want to go through this stuff of your mom's with me and see what you want to keep? We should take the rest to the thrift store in town. And you should have your mom's wardrobe. It'll fit in your spacious new bedroom.'

'What about all her clothes?' asked Minnie.

'Same. Go through 'em and take what you want. There's too much stuff we don't need. We should be...'

Dan hesitated, and it felt to Minnie like he couldn't bring himself to say the words, 'moving on', so Minnie said, 'de-cluttering, Dan?'

'That's it!' he said.

That afternoon they sat on the raised deck in front of cabin number one, taking a break and drinking lemonade. From this deck there was a fine open view of the jetty. They faced onto the property looking across to the other cabins, which were dotted about on the grassy slope – cabin two closer to the shore, cabin three across nearer to the car-parking space, and cabins four and five up on the rocky rise, close to the pines, overlooking the beach.

Dan spun his head dramatically to the left, and with a sharp intake of breath lifted his electric screwdriver and held it at the ready, like a weapon poised for attack, 'You hear that? Up on the trail! Something this way comes!'

'What?' asked Minnie.

'Sounds very much like a woman and a boy, walking and talking.'

'Oh, Dan!' And Connie and Billy came in to view walking down the trail, and through the posts carrying a canoe.

'Hi! Gosh, it's weird walking through that space now. It's like I just walked through the ghost of a cabin. All the energy that was in that space is still lingering. Did you feel the same, Billy?

'Nope,' he said, setting down his end of the canoe. 'We're going fishing, Minnie.' But Minnie was walking up the slope away from them towards where the old cabin had been.

'Cool,' said Dan, 'should I fire up the grill?'

Minnie wandered amongst the posts. Minnie had taken her first breath there. Her mom had taken her last. She stretched out her arms and looked up to her beautiful mountain, where she had always felt most at peace and where her mother loved to walk and sit and be. She turned to the sea and looked across at the bay where Connie and Billy were now paddling out in the canoe.

She remembered scattering her mom's ashes on the water and how, as she had looked down into the sea, crying over the side of the canoe, her salty tears dropped into the water. Part of her mom, that was always part of Minnie, became part of this sea, which was part of every sea on the planet.

Chapter Eighteen

The sunset painted thin wisps of cloud in hues of pink and gold, as the four of them sat on the deck of cabin number one, eating grilled trout. Connie and Billy had caught five fish. The cabin had a good-size deck and, like all the decks, it had a strong wooden railing all round to lean on and admire the view, or to place pretty shells gathered from the beach. Dan looked at Minnie. 'This is way smaller than we're used to, but it'll do fine 'til we build the new one, right?'

'Yeah,' said Minnie as she wolfed down the pink flesh of the fish.

It had been a busy day and Minnie was tired. The full moon was already rising above the mountains in the southwest as Dan took a swig of his beer from a bottle. A pair of magpies alighted on the wooden railing across the way on cabin number four. 'One for sorrow,' he said, 'two for joy.'

'Three for a girl, four for a boy,' continued Connie.

Back in the woods somewhere a couple of crows cawed a brief conversation between each other, *caw ... caw...* High in the pines behind Connie's cabin squirrels complained, *cheek, cheek, tututututut!*

'Are those gulls, terns, or skimmers?' asked Dan, peering at a wheeling flock of white birds with black-capped heads, circling and circling lower, before settling on the calm sea. He answered his own question. 'Gulls, I reckon.'

'And are those gannets or boobies?' asked Billy, stifling a giggle and pointing at a pair of large white birds with black-tipped wings and pale orange heads, floating out by the nearest island.

'Gannets,' said Dan. 'Boobies are rare this far north.' Which made Billy and Minnie giggle even more.

Connie twisted round and gazed up at the forest. 'Anyone hear thunder coming from the mountain?' There was a faint rumbling sound coming from up in the woods.

'Maybe an earthquake,' said Minnie, grinning.

But the low rumble stopped, fading quickly away, and they continued eating, apart from Dan who kept looking up at the mountain. A faint drumming sounded from deep in the woods.

'Ah, the distant drumming of the yellow-bellied sapsucker,' said Minnie.

'*You're* a yellow-bellied sapsucker!' said Billy inevitably.

'No, *you're* a yellow-bellied sapsucker!' replied Minnie.

'Let's *hope* that's a yellow-bellied sapsucker,' said Dan.

Connie stood and leaned on the rail looking back up at the mountain, the skies behind it a deep, darkening blue. 'Well, four days and nothing's happened,' she said. 'Maybe that's it. Maybe they've moved on. The smoke has gone, finally.'

Minnie looked away from the mountain and across the bay. There was no movement on the water – no boats to be seen, just the flock of seagulls floating in close formation on the still grey expanse of water, rising on the swell.

Minnie didn't want the Bigfoots to go. They'd looked after her when she'd fallen and hit her head, watched over her as she'd slept in the forest, and then terrified her and Dan escorting them out of the woods. She felt she understood them and that they cared about her and that the forest would be a different, lesser place if they left.

'Do you think they've been watching us move the cabin and everything?' asked Billy.

'Yes,' said Minnie, and Dan looked at her.

'Have you seen anything, Minnie?' he asked.

'No, but I reckon they've watched us from the trees up there somewhere and maybe even come down to take a look, at night...'

'Please, no!' said Billy.

'They don't mean us any harm, Billy. I know they don't,' said Minnie patting his back.

'And we don't mean them any harm,' said Connie.

'The more you keep your rifle out of sight, Dan,' said Minnie, 'then the closer they will come.'

Dan opened another bottle of beer, tossing the cap on the table. 'Well, I have to say that there may be something out there, but until I see one clearly, and I mean *clearly*, then I can't, hand on heart, say they exist.'

'Wow,' said Minnie, 'after all that's happened, Dan?'

'Yup. I need to see one. Just one.'

'Dan, come on!' said Connie. 'They put pine resin on her cuts!'

'Listen,' said Minnie. And they did listen – a

silence had fallen on the nearby forest. The chattering and chirping had ceased.

'That's odd,' said Connie.

'What's that?' said Billy, pointing to the furthest corner of the deck from where they were sitting. There was a small black object lying on the edge of the deck.

Minnie stood up and took a step towards it. 'It's a crow,' she said, 'and I think it's … it's dead.'

The crow was lying on its back, motionless with its black talons curled up, closed tight. They all stood up to get a better look at it.

'Is it dead?' asked Minnie, moving slowly towards it and crouching down to look more closely, but in a few seconds the bird twitched, flapped one wing, and staggered to its spindly black feet. It cawed. They all stepped back to give it space.

'Caw-Caw? Is that you?' asked Minnie, 'What's up with you?' It flapped its wings a couple of times, cawed again and lifted into the darkening sky, flying up and up towards the forest.

They all watched it, astonished by what they'd just witnessed. Connie spoke first. 'How? … What? … I've never seen such a thing.'

From below the front of the raised wooden deck where they were sitting, below the corner where the crow had been lying moments before, came a deep guttural *grunt* followed by breathy sibilance, 'Oooshh...'

'What was...?' said Billy.

'Shhh!' said Minnie, just as the top of a huge, dark-brown, hairy, cone-shaped head rose slowly up from below the deck, until two widely spaced dark eyes, under a prominent brow, twinkled in the reflected light from the cabin. There was a V-shaped notch missing from his right ear. They all froze, not moving a muscle, as he kept rising up very, very slowly, showing first the top half of his human-like face, covered in hair apart from his broad nose and hairless grey cheeks, and then his mouth, and his hair-covered chin. They could hear his breath on each exhalation, and the smell it brought to the little deck where they sat was strong – sour, piney and earthy.

The forest being looked at each of them in turn in a perfect gaze of blankness, looking at Minnie first, then Connie, Billy, Musto, then Dan. His eyes rested again on Minnie, and she felt a stirring of recognition on some level beyond her understanding, a sense of connection, of sympathy between her and this other intelligent being.

He rose slowly up until a hair-covered chest and massive muscular shoulders came into view. Black fingers with black fingernails from one massive black hand grasped the top of the railing and long thick hairs from the arm hung down. He looked like he might start to climb up and Dan put his arms out across Billy and Minnie, either side of him, but he stopped moving, stopped rising up, releasing his grip on the top rail. He opened his hand, showing a huge, wide black palm. Then he slowly lowered, the last part to disappear being that massive black hand.

'Bye,' said Minnie. Then Billy, then Connie, then Dan, then Musto. 'Bye,' 'Bye,' 'Bye,' '*Woof*.' The hand dropped from sight.

The four humans and the dog, like statues, stared into the darkness, unable to move or speak, so utterly stunned were they all by what had just happened. After what seemed like an age, Dan took one careful silent step after another, slowly crossing to the front of the deck, and looked down. 'He's gone.'

'What just happened?' said Connie. Billy was

frozen to the spot, eyes wide, mouth open, and Minnie, grinning broadly, wept profusely.

'Thank you, thank you...' she whispered.

Dan's head whipped round. 'Wait. Can you hear that? There's movement in those bushes.'

Minnie moved to the corner of the deck nearest to where the old cabin had stood and peered up the slope into the twilight gloom. She saw it, the same very tall figure, a massive black shadow ghosting away from the back of the cabin, towards the standing posts. The Bigfoot stopped, turned and looked back, resting a hand on the top of a post. She knew in that instant that he was the one, the one in the woods who had watched her, had lifted her out of the gully when she fell, and had looked out for her as she slept in his forest; and that he was the Bigfoot who had left the seafood on the jetty, as a gift.

He looked up at the full moon and in doing so Minnie was able to see his face clearly in the moon's glow – hair growing low to a brow highlighted in a silver sheen, dark eyes, a wide nose, and more dense hair covering his high wide cheeks and chin. Longer hair hung from wide muscular shoulders and long arms. There was somehow a youthful air about the creature to Minnie, despite his size, perhaps in the boney elbows and knees. He looked at Minnie a moment longer, turned and headed away up the trail.

She hoped he understood that they'd done this for them, they'd taken down the cabin, moved their entire home, for them – just in case these Bigfoots really did have 'an ancient way' that the cabin was blocking.

Days, weeks, months and years later as she would cast her mind back to this time, she felt that in those briefest of moments as their eyes locked, she had sensed that he understood.

'There's something down on the jetty!' said Dan. 'Look!

KAAYII

Chapter Eleven

The receding tide exposed more rocks embedded in the dark grey sand. Kaayii dug around them where eddying water had left dark still pools. He found shiny dark-blue mussels, small grey limpets, and muddy white cockles.

The night-time sea was as black as ink and as cold as a mountain stream, but Kaayii loved the feeling of the water on his body. When the snows melted, the ponds on the mountain were deep enough to bathe and splash about in, and the Sasquatches would take turns to 'spring clean' the nooks and crannies of their body. This salty ocean water with the pull of the tides and the swell of the waves was something else – and the sea life was plentiful, colourful and so tasty.

He waded out deeper, swam out further and dived, feeling around the rocks and seaweed. After a few failed attempts he began to be able to tell by feel alone the best crevices in which to find shellfish. After a few hours of swimming and diving he had a collection of black-and-silver-striped oysters, pink scallops, a red sea anemone and brown clams to add to his haul.

Next he needed fish so he stood, waist high in the water, and applied his uncle's technique. It took a while but he managed to catch five, one of which he ate up greedily.

He piled the sea life on a big flat rock and when he had enough, carried them in his black leathery hands over to the wooden jetty. Looking up at the cabins he could see no lights on, and could sense no humans watching him.

It took three trips to move them all but when he'd made a pile on the wooden boards he climbed up and started to arrange them in a perfectly round circle. Kaayii took care to mark the direction of the rising and setting of the sun, positioning the fishes carefully on the strips of seaweed, placing in the centre the red spiny sea anemone.

Pleased with his work, he stood over it and hoped they would like it. He hoped they would forgive the Sasquatches for banging on their sleeping places.

The two wolves jumped up as he passed the Watcher's Place and fell in with him, sniffing at his fishy, salty, hairy legs, as they trotted along up the trail. Day was dawning and a thin mist was hanging still in the valleys and hollows. A chorus of birdsong rang through the forest as the young Sasquatch and his wolf friends made their way through stands of grass and fern, under towering redwoods, past pine and fir, and aspen, alder, cedar, birch and oak, and all the animals that couldn't fly, like the polecats, weasels, racoons and porcupines, kept a very close eye on them as they passed.

When they got up to High Ridge his father was sitting with Ahniiq. The other family group in the clan was sitting together feeding on gathered mushrooms. When his mother and his sister saw Kaayii they walked over and sat with him. His sister looked at the two wolves cautiously. They sniffed her, from top to bottom.

The wolves curled up near his feet but kept their

watchful eyes open, ever alert to the sounds, smells and new senses.

Kaayii felt a growing impatience and restlessness in his father, Taashi, and as the oldest and most respected in the group that sense was felt by all the beings gathered under the pines at the top of the mountain. He sensed too that his uncle Ahniiq was not happy with Taashi.

The wolves, aware of tension between these two huge Sasquatches lifted their heads, looked at Kaayii, communicated: *hunger*, and trotted away through the pines.

Kaayii found a place under the low boughs of a pine tree away from the others. He pulled leaves and branches over his body and slept all day, tired after the swimming.

For the first time he had watery dreams – he was diving deep with strange underwater animals, blue and white, sleek and fast, catching fish in their mouths. These ones whooshed their tail up and down, instead of side to side like fish. Other strange sea creatures visited his dreams with big round heads like mushrooms, and too many legs to count, that shot off into a towering forest of swaying brown seaweed.

He awoke as the sun was setting and hurried down the mountain. He felt drawn to the lower slopes after his visit to the shoreline, after having swum in the sea, and touched with his hands the places where the humans lived.

He plucked berries from the bushes as he walked down the trails and when he reached the clearing at the Aspen Grove, he gathered and munched on wild onion.

His uncle was in the Watcher's Place staring at the bay. When he sensed Kaayii approaching he stood up and walked away without a word or a thought, gently touching his nephew's head as he passed him.

Kaayii knew Ahniiq was sad because he did not want to be left in the forest alone to look after it, when the others left. He knew there were other clans a day or two's walk away and Ahniiq could start a new clan here, but he knew his uncle, and he knew his heart was not full of joy at the idea.

Kaayii climbed a tree and could see that down among the cabins the humans had begun collecting strangely shaped things and were arranging them on the grass. He could see the girl and the man, and they were moving back and forth, from one cabin to a smaller one, carrying things.

He sensed animal energy so he stayed up in his tree waiting for it to appear. It was his wolf friends. As they approached he grunted and they looked up. Huff barked one short greeting and Kaayii climbed down to greet them. They had blood around their snouts and had a sense of contentment about them. They settled in his nest and looked at him.

Gathering more pine boughs and tree limbs, Kaayii built up the back and sides of the nest. He collected handfuls of moss and ferns and dumped them on the wolves' heads, which made him laugh. The wolves flicked the moss off and nudged the moss and ferns into a comfortable pile. At the nearest redwood tree he gathered pieces of soft bark, pulling it free with his strong fingers, and pressing it down on the wolves' mossy pile. They licked his hands appreciatively and he stroked them enjoying the deep, warm softness of their fur.

The night passed uneventfully so he dozed with the wolves. He got up at dawn, stretching his legs and grazing on juniper berries and fern fronds. He listened to the rustling of creatures in the forest, the hooting of an owl. He wondered why his uncle didn't want to stay here in this beautiful forest.

He and the wolves explored the woods by running further than usual, away from the Watcher's Place. They chased a weasel and a raccoon for fun, and whenever they stopped to rest he pulled over a small tree and leant it against another to show other Sasquatches if they ever ventured this far, that he'd been there and that this forest already had a Sasquatch guardian.

When he sensed quartz in the ground he'd stop and scrabble about clearing the earth to see if it was a big piece or a smaller loose lump. He was committing to memory all the places where there was quartz in the forest and learning all the game trails.

They ran back along the track to the Watcher's Place and he immediately climbed the tree to see what the humans were doing. He could see the man inside the cabin, the one he and his uncle had banged on, because there was no roof. The human had taken the flat pieces of wood off the top and

Kaayii could see them stacked against the little rocky cliff.

Humans seemed to like to build things, just like Sasquatches did, but to take something apart? Well, he had never heard of such behaviour from humans before. He knew that Sasquatches take structures apart and rebuild them, but only if a human has come and moved them. So, what was this man doing? Was it because he and his uncle had touched it? Kaayii thought it might just be so they could see the stars as they lay in their bed at night.

For almost all the next day Kaayii sat and watched the people from his tree. He watched as the man started to take down the walls. The man didn't look like a Sasquatch but he was behaving like one, thought Kaayii. He wondered if the man might push over a tree next, but he knew that was never going to happen as the human was too small.

This latest development was so bizarre to Kaayii that he climbed down, found a strong stick in the leaves and whacked it against the tree three times – *knock knock knock!* A short while later there was an answering double knock from way up on the mountain – *knock knock!* Then he climbed back up.

Kaayii was still there when his father appeared and started climbing up. Kaayii told his father: *no, you're too big for this tree.*

His father dropped down and climbed another one and sat there as the tree swayed slightly under his immense weight. Looking across at his father, Kaayii could see that he too was fascinated by what the man was doing and what they could see inside the cabin without the roof. It was divided up in to smaller areas inside. There was a strangely shaped, long, white thing in the smallest area that looked like what the humans use to float around on the water, and the girl was still taking things out of this cabin and over to the smaller one.

They sat in the tree all day eating sweet strips of inner bark, watching the humans. As the sun began to set the humans stopped being interesting and his father left. Kaayii climbed down and stayed with his wolves sleeping in the Watcher's Place.

The next morning from up in his tree, Kaayii watched as the man started removing the bottom part of the cabin, taking away the flooring. When he'd finished Kaayii could see tall straight stumps standing there sticking out of the ground. The cabin had gone!

He was so astonished by what the humans had done that he was about to climb down and whack three times on his tree, when he sensed his father approaching with his uncle. They climbed straight up the two closest trees. They looked down, swaying in their lofty pines, fascinated by the sight of bare stumps where the cabin had been.

Through the patchwork of pine boughs they could see movement on the track down to the cabins. It was the older female and the boy carrying something. When they came in clear sight Kaayii saw they were holding a long, curved piece of wood, and he wondered how they had managed to make it grow that way. Kaayii himself had bent young trees so that they would grow with a distinct curve to their trunk, used as a territorial marker, but this piece of wood was different.

The woman and the boy carried it down to the shore, put it on the water, sat in it and paddled with fat sticks out across the water. The three Sasquatches watched, enthralled by what they were seeing.

The girl seemed to have stopped helping the man, and was walking up past the smaller cabin and all the things they'd put there, to where the old cabin had been. She stood there alone amongst the stumps, which were much taller than her.

She looked up at the mountain. It felt to Kaayii that she could have been looking directly at him. She raised her arms up high and wide to the mountain, and gazed up at the forest standing perfectly still. Then she turned and stretched her open arms out to the sea and stood perfectly still. That's when Kaayii understood. In that instant he knew why the humans had moved the cabin.

His father, in the next pine tree, looked across at Kaayii and his words meant, 'The ancient way is clear.'

Kaayii smiled. 'I gave sea gifts. The young one, she understands.'

Kaayii, sensing his father's gratitude felt a warm glow of pride spreading through his body, and he watched as Taashi hurried down to the lowest branch, dropping as silently as a squirrel to the forest floor. Without another word, he ran through the woods, scattering weasels, rats and mice, panicking squirrels and disturbing roosting birds, so reckless and hurried and heavy were his steps as he crashed his way through the brush, straight up the mountain.

Kaayii and his uncle Ahniiq climbed down slowly. The two wolves leapt out of the perch and fell in beside Kaayii as he strode purposefully up the trail. He took his uncle's hand. He needed to communicate something important to Ahniiq and as they walked up the trail he shared his thoughts with his uncle. By the time they reached the mountaintop his uncle was a happy Sasquatch once more.

Chapter Twelve

Kaayii could see and hear much activity in and around the Sasquatch gathering place as he approached. All the structures were being dismantled. Tree limbs that had been stacked one on top of the other were pulled and moved, dragged or carried hundreds of feet away. Tree trunks that had been arranged in 'tripods' leaning against each other, were separated and scattered and the sleeping den under the fallen redwood was being taken apart.

Kaayii took his uncle's hand and led him to his father Taashi. Kaayii spoke of his love for the forest and the animals, and of his wishes. When he finished speaking his father called the clan together with two loud short calls, 'Ah. Ah!' No one took any notice, so busy were they with their work – even little Yaluqwa was throwing twigs this way and that. He called again, louder, 'AH! AH!' They gathered around.

Taashi chose words carefully, to stress the

significance of the moment and the decisions being made. The rhythm of his words, as he gazed across the trees and the bay at the wooded island beyond, repeated in their hearts. 'Full is the joyful moon as the sleeping sun sinks beyond our forest home. Kaayii is to be guardian of this mountain.'

All the adult Sasquatches and his little sister huddled tightly together, arms holding each other close and tight, with Kaayii in the middle of the group, and the Sasquatches wept, and hummed one musical note, and repeated it over and over and over.

At dusk the Sasquatches walked down the mountain together. Kaayii held hands with his mother and sister. As they passed the Watcher's Place he told the wolves to wait there. They jumped into the nest and settled down, Huff resting his head on the female's neck.

The Sasquatches crouched in the trees behind the highest cabin, and Taashi took his son's hand. He pressed his nose and his forehead softly to Kaayii's nose and forehead and communicated love to his son. Taashi picked up two straight sticks from the ground, and Kaayii backed away from the group.

The crow landed on a cedar tree nearby, and made eye contact with Kaayii, its beady yellow eyes ever alert.

He made his way stealthily down the trail towards the first cabin, listening, looking, sensing. He felt no life energy nearby so passed it quickly. Where the next cabin had stood he paused among the posts. They were chin-high to him. He felt the energy of the life that had happened in the cabin and honoured it, humming softly.

He could hear humans talking and laughing further down the slope and, tantalisingly, the gentle slop and sigh of small waves breaking on the rocks. To be so close to the sea and not be able to swim and catch fish was hard for the young Sasquatch. He reminded himself that he had more important things to do – to look after the balance of the forest on this side of the mountain and watch the recovery of the forest on the far side, the *fire* side of the mountain.

The crow landed on his outstretched hand and he held it gently in both his huge hands, telling it to *sleep*. He waited for his father's signal and when he heard the quick steady burst of drumming sticks on wood, he crept behind the cabin where the humans were sitting, and waited. When all the creatures in the woods stopped singing and chattering he crouched down so he was below the level of the deck, crawled to the corner, and lifting the sleeping crow in one hand placed him on his back, on the edge of the deck.

Kaayii kept low and listened to the humans. He could tell from their speech they were surprised to see the crow lying on the deck and they were curious about it. He heard scrabbling and flapping, then more scrabbling of sharp talons on the wood, and a loud indignant 'caw!' He watched the crow fly away.

He grunted once, long and low, 'Oooshh…' Then he straightened up from his squatting position, slowly, and there they were – looking right at him! This was the most thrilling and strange moment in his short life. The girl, the special spirited girl, was smiling at him. The others, the woman, the man and the boy, all had their mouths open and were standing as still as a dead redwood tree. He made eye contact with the girl and was happy.

He slowly lowered himself out of sight. He heard them make the same sound, each one after the other, and the dog barked once. He crawled round the side of the cabin and, when he got to the back of it, he stood up. From behind the cabin he had a good view of his clan as they crept from bush to tree down to the shore, following the ancient migration path where the cabin used to stand. Then he silently walked up the grassy slope. At the standing stumps he turned and looked back. There she was. The girl, alone, silhouetted against the darkening grey sky, her mass of curly hair highlighted by the full moon's silver glow. She was looking straight at him. He knew at that instant that she was the one human who would always be welcome in his forest and that he would always keep her safe.

He turned and walked up the trail in the darkness, up to his wolves, to his forest, to his mountain.

MINNIE

Chapter Nineteen

Though it was almost dark there was still a shimmer of reflected sky on the water. The tide was in and the jetty was floating, securely resting on its support posts, able to rise and fall with the swell of the tide. Near the jetty was a hulking black lump that wasn't usually there. It looked like a rock or a very dense bush.

'What is that near the jetty?' asked Billy with a tremor in his voice.

'Look. There!' said Dan, pointing across to the bushes in front of the other cabins, as two large figures, really just two huge black masses, like black shadows within the shadows of the night, were moving smoothly away from behind a bush, making no sound as they ran. The moonlight struck them as they flashed between the shadows cast by the tall pines on the rocky rise and their shape was outlined briefly – a sloping head with a cone-shaped skull, huge shoulders, and long arms, as they loped swiftly and silently across the ground.

Minnie joined Dan at the top of the steps. These figures were moving down towards the jetty – huge, dark, upright figures.

'Bigfoots, Dan,' she said. The four people watching the scene unfold were stupefied, stunned into silence by what they were witnessing.

The strange black mass near the jetty slowly unfolded from its haunches and stood tall. Its head was level with the top of the lamppost. It moved with a high-stepping fluid gait, its massive arms hanging below its knees. The whole jetty structure shifted in the water, under the weight of it, making the sides of the platform roll, and dip, and heave.

Without hesitation the creature jumped off the end into the sea, making a huge splash. Another two-legged creature ran along the jetty and jumped in to the sea.

'The lights, Dan! Hit the lights!' said Connie.

'I disconnected the switch when I took the cabin down! My torch is here somewhere!' He scrabbled on the deck amongst the boxes of belongings.

More creatures were stepping out of the long dark shadows between the cabins and the water, and more were coming. Another ran along the jetty, leaping and yelling with what was either alarm or delight, into the sea.

'How many's that?' asked Dan switching on his torch.

'They are impossibly large,' said Connie.

'I've counted three and here comes another,' said Billy. 'This is *so cool!*'

'It's carrying something,' said Minnie. Dan's torch was just strong enough to illuminate one end of the jetty. There was clearly a much smaller creature clinging to the back of one them. The torch lit up the last four huge figures standing there, waiting their turn. All turned to look back at the light source and their eyes glowed red, like eight large red dots.

'Oh, good Lord,' said Connie.

Dan stepped towards the cabin door. 'No, Dan, not the gun!' insisted Minnie.

'I'm getting binoculars!' said Dan as he rushed in to the cabin. In turn each Sasquatch leapt in to the water.

'Where are they going?' asked Billy.

'To the other side. To Echo Island,' said Connie, as the eight animals, plus a young one on its mother's back, swam steadily away, splashes of spray catching in the light of the full moon.

'I've heard reports of people seeing them swimming,' said Connie. 'Swimming across the bay to the other islands.'

'Will they ever come back?' asked Minnie.

'I hope so,' said Connie.

'Me too,' said Billy.

'Me too,' said Minnie. There was a pause. They all looked at Dan staring through binoculars.

'I'm good. They can have the island.'

They were down by the jetty in the morning, Minnie, Dan, Connie and Billy. 'So the crow was a distraction. Smart,' said Dan. Minnie grinned.

'I fixed these lights myself,' Dan was standing with his tape measure by one of the posts on the jetty, 'and they are all at eight feet. The tallest ones, the biggest of the, er, creatures, they were level with these lamps.'

Minnie was inspecting the ground near the steps

down to the jetty. 'There's footprints everywhere,' she said, 'in the dust at the end of the path.'

'That smell, I will not forget in a hurry,' said Connie. 'It was *really* strong.'

'I read that they can give off a really foul stench when they want to,' said Minnie. 'Like Billy.'

'Hey!' said Billy, but he couldn't help laughing.

'I was out there on the deck most of the night,' said Dan. 'I watched to see if anything swam back this-a-way.'

Minnie asked, 'Did you hear anything? See anything?'

'No. It was real quiet. They've all gone.'

Minnie looked up at Bigfoot Mountain, and smiled a knowing smile.

Later, after Connie, Billy and Musto had gone back up to their cabin, Minnie sat next to Dan on the jetty. He was looking through his binoculars, across the water, at Echo Island. He took Minnie's hand. This had never happened before in all the years she'd known Dan and she was not sure what it meant.

'Minnie, I should never have doubted you. Somehow you knew they had a kind of ancient migration route, and we were blocking it and you were right and I was wrong, all along.' He smiled at Minnie. 'You *are* your mother's daughter and I see so much of her in you, and that has sometimes been hard for me, Minnie, but I need you, and I think you need me...'

Dan was struggling to get his words out and Minnie thought he might start crying which would be weird and *so* awkward. 'And you may just be the bravest, wisest, most exceptional young woman I've ever known. Your mom would be so very proud of you...' he squeezed her hand, '...and so am I.'

Now this made Minnie cry, which took her by surprise. She gazed at the wooden jetty where a few hours earlier eight Bigfoots plus a baby one, had run and jumped into the sea.

'Dan?'

'Yes, Minnie?'

'Can I change one letter of your name?'

KAAYII

Chapter Thirteen

The two wolves trotted out of the jagged black gap in the base of the cliff. They ran through the yellow flowers and the pale grass, then stopped and waited. The young Sasquatch emerged from the cave and ran towards them. As he passed, they fell in beside him and Kaayii stroked their smooth black heads, and they closed their eyes in appreciation.

They ran on, across the streambed, through ferns and underbrush, passing redwood, cedar, spruce and pine. They ran across and up and up, and up to the summit to the stand of pines at High Ridge, where the Sasquatches used to meet and sleep. Kaayii climbed his favourite tree, nostrils bristling and scenting, the pine resin sticking to his palms, as he heaved himself up from limb to limb, never missing his grip, at home in the tree as it swayed.

He looked down the mountain, out over the tops of the trees at the water, and the hilly green island lying long and low, lit in a blaze of sunshine near the far side of the bay – far but not too far away, as the crow flies.

MINNIE

Chapter Twenty

The next day Minnie was perched high, high, high up in her favourite tree, swaying gently in the breeze with Dan's binoculars hanging round her neck by slim leather straps. She raised them to her eyes and scanned the forested mountain. The skies were clear blue and the smoke that was over the mountain just ten days ago had all gone.

She twisted round on her perch and looked out across the bay to Echo Island. Grasping the trunk with one hand she leaned out and yelled down…

'Hey, Dad! Can we take the boat over to the island?

NORTH WESTERN
CROW

WESTERN
MOOSE

BLACK-TAILED
DEER

GOLDEN EAGLE

MOUNTAIN LION

LODGEPOLE PINE

CHANTERELLE
MUSHROOM

JUNIPER

TREMBLING
ASPEN

MAIDENHAIR FERN

DOUGLAS FIR

Acknowledgements

Great thanks to my siblings, Richard, Jo and Annabel, for your support, advice and love.

Abi Sparrow at SP Agency who read a short story, saw a novel and encouraged the big push, thank you.

Penny Thomas, and all at Firefly Press, for believing, and for who making it happen.

Jess Mason for her beautiful artwork and patience.

Wise friends who read early drafts, James Nutt, Cristiana de Melo, and Emma Lyndon-Stanford. Thank you!

And Patrick and Mairi, without whom...

At Firefly we care very much about the environment and our responsibility to it. Many of our stories, such as this one, involve the natural world, our place in it and what we can all do to help it, and us, survive the challenges of the climate emergency. Go to our website **www.fireflypress.co.uk** to find more of our great stories that focus on the environment, like *The Territory*, *Aubrey and the Terrible Ladybirds* and *My Name is River*

As a Wales-based publisher we are also very proud the beautiful natural places, plants and animals in our country on the western side of Great Britain.

We are always looking at reducing our impact on the environment, including our carbon footprint and the materials we use, and are taking part in UK-wide publishing initiatives to improve this wherever we can.